W9-BTN-880

Dear Student

Rockstar Readers at
Cotuit Library –

Dear Student

Elly Swartz

Be brave!
Be fearless!
Be You!

Delacorte Press

Visit us on the Web! rhcbooks.com

Educators and librarians, for a variety of teaching tools, visit us at RHTeachersLibrarians.com

Library of Congress Cataloging-in-Publication Data
Names: Swartz, Elly D., author.
Title: Dear student / Elly Swartz.
Description: First edition. | New York : Delacorte Press, [2022] |
Audience: Ages 10 and up. | Summary: "A girl with social anxiety becomes the secret voice of the advice column in her middle school newspaper"— Provided by publisher.
Identifiers: LCCN 2020050123 (print) | LCCN 2020050124 (ebook) |
ISBN 978-0-593-37412-2 (hardcover) | ISBN 978-0-593-37413-9 (library binding) |
ISBN 978-0-593-37414-6 (ebook)
Subjects: CYAC: Anxiety—Fiction. | Advice columns—Fiction. |
Friendship—Fiction. | Middle schools—Fiction. | Schools—Fiction.
Classification: LCC PZ7.1.S926 De 2022 (print) | LCC PZ7.1.S926 (ebook) |
DDC [Fic]—dc23

The text of this book is set in 12.15-point font.
Interior design by Jen Valero

Printed in the United States of America
10 9 8 7 6 5 4 3 2 1
First Edition

To Scott and Daniel—

Big brothers are the best! I love you guys!

1

Six Postcards Ago

I thought making Dad's famous cheese eggs in our temporary home could make my life feel like it did before he left six postcards ago. Like cheese eggs for breakfast on my first day at Hillview Middle School could make everything feel normal.

But I was wrong. Nothing feels normal.

This morning, Dad video called. Another not-normal thing. I dragged my beanbag over to my computer. He looked like Dad, but not really. He was supertan and his usual short brown Dad-hair was in a ponytail.

I thought he called because he missed me. Because he wanted to wish me luck in sixth grade. But really it was about seizing the day. He had on his no-kidding face. The same one he had on the day he told me he was joining the Peace Corps. He said he felt this was something he had to do. Something he'd always talked about doing and was finally brave enough to do. Mom said she supported him. But I'm not a hundred percent sure that's still true. Sometimes I hear her crying in her room late at night.

"Autumn, this year I want you to get involved in one thing at school," he said.

I stared at my dad. "Are you seriously parenting me from halfway around the world on my first day of school?"

"Just one thing," he repeated.

"You don't get to do this. You left. Remember?"

"No matter where I live, I'm still your dad."

"Dads don't leave," I said, staring at the cheese eggs I wasn't eating.

"This is temporary," he said, like that makes it better.

I was quiet for a bit. Then I asked, "Why do I have to do one thing? I'm not you. You made your choice. Your one thing. And it wasn't us."

He sighed. Loudly.

"It wasn't me."

"I love you, Autumn. I told you leaving was never about you or Pickle or Mom. It was about finding the courage to do something that can make a real difference in the world."

I didn't say anything.

Because what he didn't get was that he didn't have to leave to make a difference.

"Seizing the day will be good for you. I promise."

I folded my arms across my sloth T-shirt. "What's good for me is having a dad who lives in the same home or state or country," I said, his latest postcard tucked into my pocket.

"I'm sorry, Autumn." His voice cracked.

And a sadness settled into my heart.

Because no matter how mad I am that he left, I'm sadder that he's gone. So I inhaled all my unspoken words and said, "Got it. One thing."

My little sister, Pickle, sneezes, and my brain jolts me back to the nerves climbing up my spine as we walk to our first days of school. It's hot and my hand is sweaty, but Pickle holds on tight. Then I see it. A beautiful baby iguana sitting in the middle of the road. I wipe my sticky forehead and lean in.

"What's he doing here?" she asks, her lime-green cape flying behind her. I made it for her right after Dad left. She told me she was scared of the monsters living under her bed. So I found some fabric in the basement, cut out a cape, and told her it had superpowers that could squash the scared-in-the-belly feelings that twist in your heart when you're supposed to be sleeping. It doesn't do anything for the feelings that come from being left behind, but I didn't tell her that.

"Not sure. But he has to be lost," I say, tucking the loose strands of brown hair back into my braid. "Iguanas don't live on the Cape."

"Where's his home?" she asks, her pigtails bouncing.

Before I can answer, a kid on a bicycle speeds toward us.

"Watch out for—" I yell.

The blue bike brakes.

Tires screech.

Time slows.

But it's too late.

Pickle screams. My braid swings and my orange high-tops slap the hot pavement as I run into the road.

The boy on the blue bike stops. Pickle and I hover over the green iguana. Its long, striped tail is bleeding.

The boy looks at us. "I didn't see him." He's out of breath. His hands fly in the air. "I mean, what's an iguana even doing here?" His face is blotchy red and he smells like peanut butter. "I'm really sorry," he says, staring at his flip-flops.

Pickle hugs my leg and starts to cry.

"Is he yours?" the boy asks me.

I swallow hard. "No," I say, looking down at my four-legged friend. His body is the color of kiwi, but his eyes are black with the tiniest rim of sunburst yellow.

"Is he going to be okay?" Pickle asks.

I bite my lip. The answer to that is knotted behind the mountain of fear shooting up from my sneakers. But I squeeze my sister's hand and nod. "Don't be scared, Pickle. We have your superpowers. Remember, superheroes come in all sizes." I cross my fingers and hope she believes me. "But now, I need your cape."

Snot leaks from her button nose as she unties her cape and hands it to me.

"We have to get him to Hillview Vet," I say, carefully wrapping the iguana in the cape.

"How far is that?" the boy on the bike asks.

"Just a few blocks back that way," I say, noticing his I LOVE CAPE COD T-shirt. Then I point in the direction we just came from. "Our mom's the vet there. It's next to Banana Splitz Ice Cream Shack."

I hold my breath and hope that sounds normal.

Like something a sixth grader would say.

Not weird. Like something no one would ever say.

"I don't know where that is. I'm not from here," he says, pulling down his Washington Wizards cap. "But I'll follow you."

I nod and exhale.

Pickle wipes her tears, points to me, and says, "That's my sister, Autumn, and I'm Gracie, but everyone calls me Pickle."

Mom nicknamed her that after she ate an entire jar of sour pickles in one sitting. Without puking.

Pickle looks down at the bundle of cape. "What should we name this guy?"

"How about Superman?" I say.

2

Fearless Fred

We sprint down the street, passing Ken's Auto Body Shop and Rudy's Cafe. The smell of coffee fills the air. I hold Superman close. I can feel my heart pounding as I run past Rigley's Market and turn right at the sign that says BEAUTIFUL YOU—NOW HIRING. Then left on Jupiter Road. Speed past Banana Splitz and burst through the big yellow front door of Hillview Vet holding an iguana wrapped in a cape.

"What happened?" Malcolm asks, scratching his bald brown head as he gets up from behind the check-in desk. Malcolm's been managing Hillview Vet since before I was born. He's more family than employee. But my hands-down favorite thing about Malcolm is that he makes the best strawberry banana cream pie ever.

The boy with the blue bike steps up. "I, um, ran him over. By accident. I was riding my bike down the hill on Oakland. And then he was just there in the middle of the street. But I didn't see him. I mean, not until after," he says, his voice cracking.

Malcolm puts his ginormous leathery hand on the boy's shoulder. "Okay. Breathe, big fella." Malcolm cradles Superman, goes back over to the desk, and calls for help. "We'll take good care of him."

Before I can ask how, Mom's standing next to me. Her T-shirt is covered in rabbit fur. She's been taking care of two rabbits who were left in a box on the doorstep of Hillview Vet last week. That happens a lot. Four days ago, it was a bearded dragon I named Flame.

"Let me take this guy," Mom says, stuffing her long, curly red hair into a silver clip on top of her head.

"His name's Superman," Pickle tells her.

Mom kisses my little sister's head and leans in to me. She smells like vanilla. And bunny.

"Is he going to be all right?" the boy asks, his freckled face turning the color of mayonnaise.

"I'll know more after I get a good look at him. Hoping

it's a just a tail wound that we can fix with a few stitches." She smiles at him. "Is he yours?"

The boy takes off his hat and I can see his spiky blond buzz cut. Then he shakes his head. "No, ma'am. He was just sitting in the road."

"You can hang out," Mom says to the boy, pointing to the waiting room. "I'll update you as soon as I know more." Then she turns to Pickle and me. "You guys need to get to school."

My stomach drops to the ugly brown-speckled floor. I try to act normal. Like I'm not terrified to start sixth grade as the girl who had to move because her dad chose to live somewhere on the other side of the world. The girl who now shares a room with her little sister.

"I don't want you to be late for your first day," Mom continues. Ever since Dad left, it's my job to get Pickle and me to school. Actually, it's my job to do a lot of things Dad used to do.

I look at the boy in his Washington Wizards cap and I LOVE CAPE COD T-shirt and think how lucky he is to be a tourist. And not to be headed to his first day of middle school.

"Mom, we can't leave Superman now. We need to know he's going to be okay. Besides, there's still time before school officially starts, and if you drive us, we can get there superquick." I look at Pickle, whose curly red pigtails bob as she nods.

Mom sighs a mix of frustration and concession. I recognize it. She did the same thing when I told her I wanted a pet of my own for my birthday last year. It wasn't long after Dad left for the Peace Corps.

And now I have a very fat, very orange guinea pig named Spud.

Mom nods, and then she and our four-legged superhero disappear into an exam room in the back. Last week, she let me come in with her when she removed glass from a falcon's claw. But today, I head to the sea of red plastic chairs in the waiting room.

The walls are covered with photos of all the animals she's treated. My favorite is the one of Sugar the tarantula, who's a lot cuter than I imagined a tarantula could ever be.

Pickle tucks her small hand into the boy's and walks him over to the table with the half-completed toad puzzle. I stare at my sister. It's so easy for her to talk to anyone and be comfortable with everyone. I wonder if she got that from Dad. She definitely didn't get his baking skills. I got those. Before Dad became Seize the Day Dad, we used to bake the best chocolate whoopie pies with the most amazing creamy goodness in the middle. We'd eat them for breakfast whenever Mom had the morning shift at Hillview Vet. She's not a fan of dessert for breakfast. But I am.

I'm not, however, a fan of Fearless Fred. That's what Dad calls the part of each of us that fear can't boss around. The part of us that, he says, takes after the bravest man he knew, Papa Fred, his dad.

The first time I heard about Fearless Fred was in kindergarten. It was my turn to share at morning meeting. I was the last kid to go and I didn't want a turn. But Dad said I couldn't let fear stop me. On my day to share, he came with me. We handed out the whoopie pies we'd made together the night before and then I was supposed to talk about them. But the words stuck like glue to the back of my throat. Nothing came out but a long beat of loud silence. Dad inched closer to me, smiled, and nodded. I took in a giant breath of brave and told my classmates how we baked the whoopie pies. When we got home, Dad said I found Fearless Fred, and that's what we've called it ever since.

I grab a plastic chair and pull out my notebook with the orange-and-purple-check cover. It was the last thing Dad gave me before he left. I slip off the rubber band that's holding the frayed pages together and take out the first postcard from him. My heart tugs. On the front is a photo of two smiling girls about my age hugging a giant brown dog.

Dear Autumn,

Meet Lucia and Maria! They're part of my host family, along with their mom and dad. And that's Bruno, their two-year-old mutt.

The girls remind me so much of you and Pickle. Lucia loves to write. Just like you! I miss you both so much. And no matter where I am, know that I'm sending love.

I promise to send postcards and call and text.

Remember to seize the day!

Your Loving Dad

I run my fingers across his handwriting. It's weird how much I love the way he writes my name. Especially his loopy *A*. This postcard came just a few weeks after he got to Ecuador. It was supposed to make me happy. But mostly it made me feel replaced.

"What's that?" the boy with the buzz cut who ran over the iguana asks, peeking over my shoulder.

My brain freezes. Thankfully, my body doesn't. I slap my notebook closed. "Nothing," I say as I kick off my sneakers to let my toes breathe.

Then the boy points to the ceiling. "Nice chicken."

Hanging above us is one of the many weird gifts my mom has received from grateful patients. It's a stuffed chicken from Mr. and Mrs. Frankel to thank her for saving their favorite porcupine. I wonder what they would have sent if she'd saved their least favorite porcupine.

I smile, and before I can figure out a not-weird thing to say, Pickle jumps onto my lap and turns to our waiting-room friend. "Do you have a pet?"

He nods. "Yep. A dog named Mr. Magoo."

Pickle laughs. "That's a funny name." Then, "What's your favorite color? Mine's green."

"Um, blue," he says.

"What's your favorite food?"

"Peanut butter."

Pickle hops off my lap and starts skipping around the room. "Who's your favorite superhero?"

"This is a hard one," the boy says. "I'm going with Flash."

"He's okay," Pickle says. "But I like Wonder Woman best."

"Good choice." He smiles.

Not sure if it was at me or just in my direction. But I notice his dimple.

My thoughts scramble when a big black dog runs into the room wagging his tail.

"That's Bear," Malcolm calls from the front desk. "He's mine."

The boy leans over and Bear licks his face again and again. We all laugh.

Then the boy's eyes dart toward the clock on the wall. He stands. "I'm really sorry about the iguana. But I've got to go."

"Wait. You can't leave now. We don't know what's going to happen to Superman," I say.

And I liked talking to you.

He turns and looks back at me. His face full of sorries. "I'd stay if I could," he says. Then, just like that, the boy with the blue bike and buzz cut who ran over the iguana walks out of Hillview Vet.

3

Just Some Kid

He's just some kid I won't ever see again.

This happens every summer. Families pour onto my Cape in their SUVs stuffed with beach chairs and boogie boards and bikes. I see them at King's Beach in their I LOVE CAPE COD T-shirts and hats, collecting shells and sunbathing on unicorn floats. They bring their sick frogs and hamsters and rabbits to Mom. Then, when school starts, we stay and they leave. Just like the boy on the blue bike.

It's fine. We were just two people in the same space who didn't even know each other. We weren't friends.

But for a moment I thought we could be.

I shake away the disappointment that comes with

being left, and go online to find out more about iguanas. Turns out they're good swimmers and usually live near water in warmer climates nowhere near Massachusetts. So what was this guy doing in the middle of the street on the Cape?

I look at the empty chair where the boy was sitting and wish Prisha still lived here. She'd know. Or at least help me figure it out. But as of the middle of July, she's been living in sunny California. Prisha and I were supposed to conquer middle school together. We were actually supposed to conquer everything together. But Prisha came over one Saturday morning with wet cheeks and puffy eyes. Her mom was promoted to some big position in her company and they were moving to California. I hugged my best friend and tried not to show the heap of sadness that filled my insides.

I know how hard it is to move. When Dad left, money was tight. At least, that's what I overheard Mom telling Malcolm. So we moved from the house I love with the lilac bushes we planted in the yard to the small apartment above Hillview Vet with no lilacs and a room I share with Pickle and Spud.

Mom says it's temporary. Just until Dad comes back to his accounting job. And us.

What Mom doesn't get is that temporary doesn't make any of it hurt less.

So now I have no one to help me figure things out. And no one to walk into Hillview Middle with today. Unless I find a superpower that can clone Prisha or make Spud invisible so I can sneak him into school. I'm open to either.

While Mom's still with Superman and Pickle's happily coloring next to me, I open my laptop and find the school's newspaper—*The Express*.

The front page is about welcoming the sixth graders, announcing the new panini press in the cafeteria, and tips on how to make the most of the school year. My stomach twists.

The next section has the schedule for sports tryouts and theater auditions. I keep going.

On the last page is what I'm looking for. The Dear Student letters. They're kind of legendary at Hillview Middle. Each year, one student from sixth, seventh, or eighth grade is selected by Mr. Baker—my advisor and English teacher—to be the voice of Dear Student. No one knows which grade he's selecting from or the ultimate identity of that person. It's all a big mystery. Then kids write in their questions and problems, and the secret student replies with advice. It's hands-down the best part of the paper.

I didn't ask Dear Student for advice. But now with Prisha in California, Dad still in Ecuador, and me living in a temporary apartment with no lilacs, I'm wondering if I should have.

I click open the letters.

Dear Student,

The fall dance is soon and I don't know if I should wear my favorite cowboy boots with the fringe or my checked Vans to match my best friend. She wants to go as shoe twins.

Sincerely,
Undecided

I didn't even know there was something called shoe twins.

Dear Undecided,

Be you. Wear the boots.

Sincerely,
Student

Dear Student,

Feeling kinda lost. Could use some help finding my courage to, you know, just be. Yo, can you help me?

Sincerely,
Frightened

Dear Frightened,

You're braver than you realize. I promise.

Sincerely,
Student

Dear Student,

Need to know! If you were on an island and could only bring one food, what would it be?

Sincerely,
Peanut Butter (my food of choice)

Dear Peanut Butter,

Ha! Good choice, but I'd settle on chocolate donuts.

Sincerely,

Student

Pretty sure I'd bring whoopie pies. The kind Dad and I make. Or used to make. The night before he left, we baked our favorite vanilla cream whoopie pies. And that was our last time baking together or doing anything together for a long stretch. My heart slides a beat. I wonder if seizing the day always feels this way.

At the end of the last letter, there's a box:

ALWAYS WANTED TO BE THE SECRET VOICE OF DEAR STUDENT?

NOW'S YOUR CHANCE!

EMAIL MR. BAKER
AND TELL HIM WHY YOU WANT THE JOB!

And a shout-out of thanks to last year's secret advice columnist.

Today's release wraps up their term.

4

Our Forever Home

I've thought about asking Dear Student for advice, but I've never thought about *being* Dear Student. I wonder what it would feel like to be the secret voice. To give advice. To people. About stuff.

Maybe *this* could be my one thing.

I look at the Dear Student ad again.

I used to give Prisha advice. She said I was super-good at it. Like the time I taught her bulldog, Brando, how to ring a bell when he needed to go outside to pee. Or when I told her to shake a cup of pennies to stop him from stealing her retainer.

But what if kids want to know about other things? Not just dog stuff.

What if they hate the advice I give?

My stomach knots and I close the paper.

A girl with two red bows walks into the vet office with a cage filled with baby mice. She sits down next to me. "Aren't they cute?"

Cute isn't exactly the adjective I'd use to describe the pink hairless pile of babies, but if I'm in-my-heart honest, she might get mad. I learned that when Chloe Brown asked me at the beginning of fifth grade if I liked her new haircut. I didn't. I told her not to worry because it would grow out and she could totally pull off a bad haircut. She stopped talking to me.

So, I nod. Bows smiles big and practically skips to the desk with her dad when Malcolm calls their name.

When Bows is gone, I look up mice online. Baby mice. Turns out their rear teeth never stop growing, like Spud's front teeth.

I open my notebook and the words spill out of my brain about a girl named Kiko with a pet iguana, Apollo, who loses his tail, and when it grows back, it has the power to make the girl invisible. That's how it happens. Stories find me. Then I shut out the world, listen, and write. On the page, I don't worry and the words don't stick.

"Superman is going to be okay." It's Mom. I stop writing.

"What was he even doing there?" I ask.

"Maybe someone lost him," she says.

I think about how I'd feel if I lost Spud and am thankful I made him a tiny orange collar with his name and Hillview Vet's telephone number embroidered on it.

"I put a photo of Superman on our website and on all our social media pages. I'm sure someone will claim him," Malcolm says.

"What happens now?" I ask.

"This guy will stay here until he gets better, so we can check on him and make sure he's healing properly."

"Do you think he still needs my cape's superpowers?" Pickle asks.

"You were so brave to share it with him," Mom says, tucking her curls behind her ear. "It's yours again just as soon as I clean it."

Worry splashes across Pickle's round face. "But I really need it for school."

"I promise to bring it to you as soon as it's clean," Mom says. She looks around the waiting room. "Where did the boy who came in with you go?"

I shrug. "He said he had to leave."

We pile into Mom's tan truck and drive over to Hillview Middle School. It's where all three elementary schools from our town come together to make one big Falcon Family. That's what Principal James said in his welcome-to-sixth-grade letter.

I rub my *hamsa* charm for good luck. It was Grandma Bea's, then Mom's, now mine. Mom gave it to me after we moved to our apartment. She said Grandma brought it back from Israel to protect and watch over her. It's beautiful, with all different shades of blue and an eye etched into the palm of an open hand. Mom said it was filled with generations of love and would watch over me no matter where I lived.

I rub it one more time and hope it helps with the stack of worries that comes with a new school, temporary things, and being left behind.

5

Five Things

Mom parks the truck and reaches over to hug me. I stare at my mother in her shirt covered in rabbit fur.

My shoulders squeeze.

“Mom, not here.” I open the door. “I’m late—I’ve gotta go,” I say, like my heart isn’t racing and my hands aren’t sweating. Last night, Pickle walked over to my bed and whispered in my ear, “I can’t find Fearless Fred.” She blinked back a tiny tear. I held her hands and told her when I can’t find Fearless Fred, I close my eyes and imagine myself doing the brave thing and try again. I didn’t tell her that it doesn’t always work.

"Have the bestest first day," Pickle says, jarring me back.

"You too. And don't worry, you'll be great." I reach into my bag and take out a small, lime-green felt heart and hand it to my little sister.

She gives me a piece of paper folded into a triangle. "This is for you."

When I open it, there's a picture in green and orange crayon of two girls holding hands. And wearing capes.

"I love it."

I put the drawing in my notebook, grab my guinea pig backpack, close the door of the truck, and walk into my first day of middle school.

Alone.

My single braid falls over my shoulder. This morning, I wove in the orange ribbon that Prisha gave me when she moved. Prisha had worn it in her licorice-black hair every day. It was silky soft and left over from a sari her nani had been sewing. It had been one long piece until the morning we said goodbye. Then Prisha cut it in two, gave me half, and said, "This way we can be together even when we're apart."

Mom said she liked the way it looked woven into my braid. Which made me nervous because she's also the one who wears khaki pants every day and calls me a gentle spirit, like that's a good thing.

I walk down the hall, passing a few other stragglers. Lost or late, like me.

I try to look like I'm not terrified to be here.

But the more normal I pretend to be, the less normal I feel.

By the time I check in at the office, there are drops of sweat sliding down the sides of my face. The woman at the desk with the short blue hair offers me a box of tissues. I grab a handful and she sends me to Room 707. The halls are lined with lockers and signs that say WELCOME! to make us feel like middle school is a happy place.

It's not working.

I touch the *hamsa* that's dangling from the chain around my neck, take a ginormous breath of air, and walk into my classroom. Mr. Baker's standing at his desk in a BELIEVE IN YOURSELF T-shirt. I met him on Step-Up Day at the end of fifth grade. We got a tour of the school and he gave us donuts. I remember him and the donuts, but unfortunately, I don't recall where anything is in this huge place.

"It's going to be a fantastic year!" he says like he's president of the Feel Good at School Committee. He points to an empty desk in the second row. I don't look at the eyes staring at the girl coming in late. I cross my fingers behind my back and hope Mr. Baker's right.

He sits on his desk, his black-and-red sneakers hanging over the edge. "Okay, first, the boring stuff." He tells us how to read our schedules, the cell phone policy, where to find our lockers, and how to open them. Which is good since that part kind of freaks me out.

"Now that we've got that out of the way, on to the good stuff." He smiles. "Who's ready to share their writing?" It was our day one assignment. He emailed it to us two weeks ago and said we could write about anything we wanted.

I lay my arm across my orange-and-purple-check notebook. I'm going to turn in my new story about Kiko and Apollo instead of the one I wrote last week about hermit crabs, but I don't want to share out loud. Not today. My fingers touch the cover and I lift the frayed edges.

I don't raise my hand. Instead, I look around at the unfamiliar faces with name tags on their shirts and hands in the air. My heart pounds so loudly I worry the boy next to me with the pimple in the middle of his forehead might not be able to hear Jamal reading his story about a pod of evil drones that take over a summer camp and Sophie sharing about the first-ever female referee in the NFL.

When Sophie's done, I smile like I was listening.

Mr. Baker tugs on his beard as he talks about what we'll be reading and then says, "I want to get to know each one of you. So tonight, your assignment is to tell me five things." In big letters he writes on the whiteboard:

1. SOMETHING ABOUT YOURSELF
2. SOMETHING ABOUT YOUR FAMILY OR NEIGHBORHOOD
3. SOMETHING YOU LOVE TO DO
4. SOMETHING YOU HATE TO DO
5. SOMETHING YOU WANT TO LEARN

A boy named Juan raises his hand. "Is this like an essay?"

Mr. Baker shakes his head. "You can answer these questions any way you'd like. Writing. Drawing. Video." He walks around the room. "I just want your answers to reflect who you are." He stops and smiles. "And don't forget, the club fair is this week."

The girl two seats over with the cool black-rim glasses and sparkly sneakers says, "The club fair is going to be epic."

I stare at her, wondering if joining a club is what kids do in middle school.

Mr. Baker continues. "I run the school newspaper and have a few spots that need to be filled for both the online and paper versions, if any of you are interested."

My mind flips back to Dear Student. There's a speck of me that still thinks I should apply. That maybe it should be my one thing.

Mr. Baker finishes with, "Have a great rest of your day, and don't forget to take a map of the school on your way out. This place is big and can be confusing."

I grab my backpack, and as I stuff my books and notebook inside, Pickle's card falls onto the floor. Open. Two girls. Green and orange crayon. Holding hands. Wearing capes.

My eyes pop as a wave of nausea shoots across my chest.

I reach down to pick up the drawing, but it's already in someone else's hand.

My body freezes.

I look up. It's Mr. Baker. He folds the paper, smiles with the gentlest eyes, and hands it back to me.

I exhale, put Pickle's drawing in my backpack, and head to Spanish class. I started taking Spanish in fourth grade with Prisha when her mom took a job teaching English to parents who only speak Spanish. Now Prisha takes French in California and I'm heading to Spanish by myself.

I wind through the hall to my right, only to realize I went the completely wrong way. I look at Mr. Baker's map, but it doesn't help because I have no idea where I am. It feels like someone squeezed all the air out of the hall. It takes me three tries and forever to find my class. Señora López is already taking attendance when I slide in late next to a boy in the front row. The only seat left.

The boy turns my way. His eyes widen.

My breath catches in the back of my throat.

It's the boy with the buzz cut and the blue bike.

The one I thought was a tourist.

The one who ran over Superman.

6

Table of Strangers

The boy with the buzz cut shifts in his seat.

Uh-oh. Should I wave?

His eyes are brown.

Say hi?

I swallow hard.

Tell him Superman's okay?

While I'm deciding the least embarrassing option, he spins away from me and now all I see is the back of his head.

We go across the room, which feels burning hot and too small, and share our English names and get our Spanish ones. Turns out the boy with blue bike's name is Cooper in English *and* Spanish.

Why didn't he just say he had to leave to go to school?

Doesn't matter. Because I can't ask. I don't know how to say any of that in Spanish. And Señora has a strict no-English policy. That she told us in English.

Señora's dark eyes turn my way. "¿Cuál es tu nombre?"

I know that means *What's your name?* "Mi nombre es Autumn," I say softly.

"Aw, what a beautiful name," Señora says to me. "Autumn or *Otoño,* like the season."

I feel my face turn beet red and hope the boy named Cooper isn't looking at me.

After Spanish, I sprint to math to get away from the flood of confusing thoughts. I try to focus on what Ms. Scott is saying about fractions, but my mind is still spinning from seeing Cooper. Here. At my school.

When the bell finally rings, I'm thankful it's lunch. My stomach has been embarrassingly loud grumbling for the last twenty minutes. But as I walk into the cafeteria and grab my tray, my nerves weave their way up my spine. This place is humongous and filled with piles of kids. The tables are long and crammed next to each other. The bright lights buzz above my head. To my right is a table filled with kids from my old elementary school. Shannon and Xavier and Luciana smile. I give a small wave, trying not to drop my lunch tray. I see the boys who used to play basketball on the hardtop at the table to my left. I don't spy Cooper anywhere.

I look around and have no idea where the line starts. Kids are moving in all directions, and I feel like I'm the only one who can't figure it out. My heart rapid-fires. I inhale to find my calm, but it's not working. Finally, I spy the french fries. Now, to get to them and a burger and hopefully dessert without bumping into any trays full of food. The last thing I want to be is the girl who knocked over someone's lunch. I carefully step in line behind a kid with pink hair and a nose ring and wish I could teleport anywhere else. My stomach grumbles again. The food actually smells good. Which is a happy surprise. But this place makes me feel like I did that time at Tubes of Wonder.

It was my 6th birthday celebration. Pickle was a newborn, so we weren't technically sharing our birthdays yet. There were tubes to crawl through, a ball pit to hide in, and lots of Skee-Ball. That was the first time I can remember feeling happy and not-so happy at the same time. Mom said that can happen sometimes. Which is confusing, but true.

I slip the food onto my tray, but now I have no idea how to pay for it. I remember Baker saying something about an account. I hope that's true because I'm superhungry and didn't bring any money with me. The woman at the end of the line with the hairnet tells me to swipe my ID.

I cringe.

I hadn't realized that Step-Up Day was also photo day. So my hair in my picture looks like a cross between Albert Einstein's and Medusa's. I fumble for it in my backpack as the line grows behind me. I try to ignore the grunts and are-you-kidding-mes as I pull out my folders and notebooks until I find my ID floating at the bottom of the bag. I slide it through the card reader, stuff it quickly back into my bag, and turn to leave the cafeteria, when the girl from class with the cool glasses and sparkly sneakers walks up.

"Hey, aren't you in Baker's class?" she asks, running her hand over her blond braids.

I nod.

"I'm Logan," she says.

"Autumn," I say, as I watch the boy behind her guzzle an entire Yoo-Hoo.

She points to a table filled with girls who are waving her over. Girls who I don't know. "Want to eat with us?"

I freeze. The part of me that's scared to do middle school alone wants to scream yes. But the part that feels awkward is nervous I'll say something dumb. "I was going to, um, maybe eat." I pause and look around. "Not here."

She grabs my hand like we're forever friends. "Don't be stupid. Why wouldn't you eat in the cafeteria? I mean, that's why they built this gigantic place. Right?"

I nod like there isn't a prickly feeling climbing up my body. Like I don't remember Mickey Ray standing on his chair in first grade and calling me a weirdo in front of the whole cafeteria.

I tuck in my worries and follow Logan to the table of strangers.

"This is Autumn," she announces as I set down my tray holding a cheeseburger and fries and piece of chocolate cake.

Waves and smiles. And salads. Everyone but me is eating greens. Just greens.

Maybe I should have grabbed the Caesar. But I look down at my lunch and am happy I didn't.

Logan puts a sheet of paper in the middle of the table. "I found a list of all the clubs we can choose from," she says, excitement bouncing off her words. "Plus, there's the Dear Student thing."

"Are you going to apply?" a girl in a lilac shirt asks.

"Totally," Logan says. Then she turns to me, "What about you? Will you apply?"

All eyes land on me.

I ignore the tiny part of me that's still thinking about it and shake my head.

"But check this out," Logan says, pointing to Your Voice Matters. "It's the best club. Does all kinds of social-action stuff." She pours dressing on her salad and looks my way. "You have to do this one with us. Please." She pushes up her glasses and the girls around the table nod.

I try to find Fearless Fred.

The one who's not scared to say anything.

But the words are lost. So I dunk my fry in ketchup and mustard, and wish I had Kiko's invisibility superpower.

7

Spud and Flame and Maybe Superman

When I walk into Hillview Vet after school, Pickle's already there. She runs over. "My green felt heart has superpowers."

I smile.

"It brought me good luck today."

"Really?"

She nods. "Our class has a fuzzy brown hamster named Cinnamon. And my teacher said we could have a Superhero Day where we wear capes and tell everyone our superpower. Mine's going to be that I can stay underwater like a frog for a really long time."

She starts hopping and croaking.

"How was your first day?" Mom asks, kissing the top of my head.

"On a scale of one—being bitten by a tarantula—to ten—Prisha moving back, it was a solid five and a half," I say, which is mostly true.

"I also told my teacher that our birthdays are soon," Pickle says. "I'm going to ask Kamal and MaryLou and the boy down the street who doesn't talk a lot to come to Hillview Vet for chocolate cupcakes with extra sprinkles."

"Sounds great," I say.

"Who are you going to invite?"

Pickle and I share a birthday. We were born exactly six years apart. Well, not exactly. I was born at 10:10 at night and she was born at 4:20 in the afternoon. But the same date. So, for almost six years, we've shared our chocolate-cupcakes-with-extra-sprinkles birthday celebration.

"Spud and Flame and Superman," I say.

A smile erupts across Pickle's face.

And maybe Dad.

I hope seizing the day can mean coming home.

I ask Mom how Superman's doing and she tells me he's improving.

I walk to the back hall to visit my iguana friend. "You're really brave," I say as he nibbles a piece of Swiss chard. Prisha would love Superman. My heart misses her. This morning, I sent her my story. She sent back an iguana emoji and a smiley face and told me to keep going. She wants to know what happens. So I open my checked notepad and write. My letters are small. I don't want to use up all the pages until Dad comes back.

> Apollo nudged Kiko. Something was wrong. She felt it, too. It's a sense she'd had all day. At first, she thought it was the fish tacos from lunch. But when she got home, she knew it was something else. She'd had tiny glimpses of it when she first realized her new power. Like when she knew the garbage truck had run over the neighbor's fence or the refrigerator with all the chicken Mom had cooked for the block party died before she'd actually seen it. Kiko just knew. In her bones. This was like that. But bigger. Something was happening. And it wasn't good. She turned on her superpower. And went outside. Invisible from the world.

I close my notebook and water the plants growing in the pots in the greenhouse behind the front desk. I promised Malcolm I'd help keep them alive.

Pickle finds me while I'm watering the collard greens. "Will you help me? I have to read." Her usually happy eyes spark sad. "Even though I can't read."

"It's okay. I got you." She sits on my lap.

Reading with Pickle was Dad's thing. Now it's my thing.

Pickle hands me *The Secret Shortcut,* one of the best books of all time. "I think it's super-duper unfair that I have to read every day when I can't read. I'm going to ask Ms. Tanaka if I can hop instead. I'm a really good hopper."

We sit and read about pirates and crocodiles and rickety bridges. Mud and monkeys and birds with long beaks. I tell Pickle to follow along with her finger. After the third time through she starts saying some words before me and her little body wiggles with happiness.

"You're the best big sister. Maybe I won't need to hop."

Hmm. Maybe I can help some humans.

I open *The Express* again to the Dear Student letters.

I think about Dad and just one thing.

I think about Fearless Fred.

Then I click open the application. Bite my lip. Hug the part of me that thinks this is a good idea. And type.

DEAR STUDENT APPLICATION

Applicant: Autumn Blake

Why should Mr. Baker pick you to be the next great secret voice of Dear Student?

> I'm honest. I love to write. My friend who moved away says I give good advice. I'm kind of quiet. My mom says that's because I'm a gentle spirit. But I see everything. Take it all in and think about stuff. A lot. Like why Frightened was really frightened. I think I can help people. Kind of like my dad when he was around. He would have been a great secret-advice person. Except he's gone now.

I take in a big breath of waiting-room air and hit Send.

8

No Sixth Grader in the History of Sixth Graders

I sit and wait for something to happen. Something big.

Like the world knows I applied. Like it's blowing up balloons, tossing confetti in the air, and celebrating my maybe-one thing. My seizing the day. My Fearless Fred.

But nothing happens.

So I run upstairs to the apartment and call Prisha to celebrate. She doesn't start school until tomorrow and I figure she's outside the fringe of secrecy since she lives thousands of miles away in a different time zone.

"You'd be so good at that," she says. "Remember how great you were when the tarantula was sick? And how you helped Pickle not be scared, with the cape?"

I nod even though she can't see me.

"And the time you sent me a tiny paper star and a box of fire-hot jawbreakers when I was homesick at camp?"

I laugh and pick up the photo of Prisha and me from our Day of Nothing. That's what we called it. We stayed in our pajamas until dinner, ate popcorn, and talked about what animal we'd be if we could morph into one. Prisha picked an emu. Which made me laugh until my stomach hurt. I picked a koala bear.

I put the photo back on my nightstand next to the one of us covered in red, green, yellow, and purple powder from the Holi Festival of Spring last year.

"You made me feel so much better. At least, until I ate too many jawbreakers and threw up."

"Does that still count as helping?"

"It does. I wasn't homesick anymore. And in a day, I wasn't puking either. I even still have the star."

"You do?" I didn't know she'd kept it.

"Yep, it's right next to the goofball black-and-white photos we took in the photo booth on the beach boardwalk last summer."

I loved that afternoon. We made a hermit crab sandcastle and ate lemon slushies from the #1 Slushie stand.

"I haven't thought about any of that stuff in a long time."

"You're good at that kind of thing. You'd make a great Dear Student."

"Thanks," I say, smiling. "I really hope I get it. And if I do, I promise not to tell anyone to eat an entire box of fire-hot jawbreakers."

Prisha laughs.

In that moment, I realize how much I miss my friend with the long black hair and skin like the gingerbread cookies we used to bake with her mom.

When I hang up with Prisha, happiness wraps around me. I have a plan and maybe even my one thing.

I get an email from Malcolm and head back downstairs to the waiting room with a mop. A bunny just pooped on the floor.

After that's cleaned up, I check on Spud, who's waddling across Malcolm's desk. "A wild goose came in injured," Malcolm says. "Your mom's checking on him."

I love animals more than anything but could never be a vet. Every time I hear about an animal who's sick or hurt, my heart slides all the way down. Like it did when our dog Rumpelstiltskin died. He was a rescue. Brown and furry and full of love, from his pink-spotted nose to his curly tail. When I left for school that morning, the sky was white with snow. I kissed our dog between his ears and said goodbye. Hours later, he was hit by a snowplow. When I was called to the principal's office and saw my parents standing there, I knew something was wrong. Really wrong.

And I was right. Rumpelstiltskin was forever gone. That day I realized that being right isn't always a good thing.

Spud's crawling up my arm when a girl with two blond braids and a flowered skirt marches in holding a turquoise travel case. It's Logan. I slip behind the wall and peek out. She doesn't see me, but I spy her sparkly sneakers. I look down at my orange high-tops and wonder if someone like Logan would think working here is weird.

"Hi," she says to Malcolm. "This is Snow White, my gravid ball python." She points to the dark chocolate brown snake with tan blotches curled up in the case. "My mom's parking the car and had to make a phone call. She'll be in soon, but I can fill out the forms or take Snow White in the back and you can just tell my mom where we went."

"I believe I spoke to your mom on the phone," Malcolm says.

"Nope, that was me." Logan smiles and I can see her super white teeth.

This is my chance. Say something.

"Great. Well, welcome to Hillview Vet," Malcolm says, handing Logan some paperwork and offering her a mint from the bowl on the desk.

"Thanks." She grabs a red-striped candy, the papers, Snow White, and heads to the waiting room that smells like bleach from the bunny clean-up.

I watch her from behind the wall.

Say, "Hi. Remember me?" That's not weird.

I lean in. She's sitting down now.

Do it. Talk to her.

My nails dig into my palms as I clench my fists tight. Count to twenty. Let go. Big breath in and out.

I walk over.

Her head's down. She's writing something on those sheets Malcolm gave her.

Wait. Maybe I'm interrupting.

I quickly turn back to the front desk, my heart racing. I pretend not to watch her but take the smallest glimpse.

She's marching back over to Malcolm.

Think of something to say. Something normal.

"Here you go." She hands Malcolm the information on the clipboard.

The words tangle in the back of my throat.

She turns toward me.

Uh-oh.

"Hey, Autumn."

I smile.

"I like your guinea pig," she says.

I smile and forget the nerves inching up my spine. "Thanks. His name's Spud." I pause. "Because he looks like a giant baked potato."

Malcolm looks up. "Dr. Blake is ready for Snow White."

Logan disappears into one of the rooms with her python.

And I'm left standing at the front desk, worried that no sixth grader in the history of sixth graders would ever name their pet after a baked potato.

9

Not Embarrassing at All

I bite my lip and look up ball pythons. I learn *gravid* means that Snow White's pregnant. I also learn that she eats thawed frozen rats and sheds her skin.

Logan and Snow White are in Exam Room 3. I quietly press my ear against the closed door but can't hear anything. I leave to see if the tomato plants need more water and come back. Lean in. Still nothing.

"What are you doing?" Malcolm asks.

"Nothing," I say, which could be true.

Even though it's not.

I *want* to accidentally run into Logan so I can say something not dumb that will erase the other embarrassing thing I've already said. But I'm not telling

Malcolm that. Before I can walk away, the door opens and Logan and Snow White walk out of Exam Room 3.

Say something.

This is your chance. Ask her why she has a python. Why it's named after a Disney princess. Why anything. Just say something.

I open my mouth.

What if middle schoolers don't ask other middle schoolers this kind of stuff?

I close my mouth.

"Wilbur needs his dressing changed if you want to help," my mother says, poking her head out from the back hall.

"Be there in a minute, Mom." Those words are not stuck.

Logan looks at me.

My body freezes. *Did I just say something else stupid?* I inhale my frustration and embarrassment.

"Dr. Blake's your mom?" Logan asks.

I nod, hoping with all the powers in Pickle's cape that's a good thing.

"Cool," she says.

My insides do the happy dance. "Thanks," I say. "I work here. Well, I did over the summer. Cleaned cages and fed the animals."

My words are out.

"Lucky!"

I smile. A real, not-embarrassing-at-all smile.

The chime on the door jingles. I look up, and it's a woman who has the same blond hair, super white teeth, and big eyes as Logan. The woman struts over to the front desk. "Hi, I'm JoJo Bellingham. I want to apologize for being late and to thank you and Dr. Blake for taking such good care of Snow White."

"It's our pleasure," Malcolm says, shaking the woman's hand.

The woman grins and drapes her arm across Logan's shoulders.

I try to think of something to say.

Hi, I'm Autumn.

Or:

Happy you could come by.

Or:

I'm a huge fan of ball pythons.

JoJo turns to me. "And who are you?"

"This is Autumn," Logan says. "The girl from school I told you about."

She told her about me.

"Her mom's the vet here."

Her words are hard to hear over the potbellied pig's loud snorts from one of the back rooms.

"Nice to meet you, Autumn."

I smile and Logan blurts out, “Do you want to come over?”

Like right now?

“Um,” I say, staring at the photo of the parakeet on the wall behind her.

“Please.” She takes my hand like we’re friends who share secrets and have sleepovers.

Don’t be weird.

“Um, maybe” slips out.

“Maybe?” she says.

Okay, that was weird.

“I mean, I just need to check with my mom.” I cross my fingers and hope kids in middle school check with their parents before making plans.

I find Mom, who says yes.

Then I go back to Logan. “Sure,” I say.

Like I’m ready.

10

Surprisingly Not Gross

We pile into JoJo's blue Prius, which she calls Bertha. Dangling from the rearview mirror is a plastic Lady Justice and a long, clear crystal that Logan says is for positive energy.

"I got that after arguing my first case in court." JoJo points to Lady Justice. "It was to demand equal pay for equal jobs. I was representing a female judge getting paid significantly less than her male counterpart for doing the same job. I keep it to remind myself how far we've come and how far we still have to go," JoJo says.

Logan nods in the front seat.

Then JoJo pats Bertha's dashboard. "She's got

174,000 miles on her. Gotten me to every case I've argued around the country. The last one was in Pennsylvania. I'm not a big flier, so I plan to keep her until she or I flat-out stop running." She laughs.

The ride's filled with Logan talking about women's rights and when they lived in Chicago and how much she misses deep-dish pizza with lots of cheese from Mack's Pies.

We turn left and pass a building with a long line of people out front. "Check that out," Jojo says pointing to the sign that says BEAUTIFUL YOU—NOW HIRING. "They're getting tons of buzz for creating new jobs in town. Let's just hope they're hiring lots of women."

We slow down and make a right down Lincoln Road. I spy my old house and its new family. There are twin girls with pigtails doing cartwheels on the front lawn. My stomach dips.

"I hope you like pizza." The words pull me back to Bertha.

I turn toward Logan, away from the window, and nod. Her house is the third ranch on Vine Street, the redbrick one with the wooden door. We park next to her dad's motorcycle and Logan tells me about his newest business idea.

"It's called Crunchy Crickets—The New Chip. Dad

says crickets are full of protein and cheap to harvest." She adds, "You should try one. They're surprisingly not gross."

My brain bursts with *would rather eat pizza.*

The hallway is sunlit and filled with newspaper photos of JoJo standing next to the women she's represented for equal pay, wrongful termination, harassment, and discrimination in the workplace. There's even a glass award on the table in front of the gray-and-white-striped couch that says WOMAN OF THE YEAR.

Logan comes over with a framed photo. "This one is of me and my mom at the Equality March in Chicago. It was amazing! Did you go to the one in Boston? I heard it was packed."

I shake my head. I remember the Equality March. We didn't go. That was after Dad left. We'd just rented our home to the family with the cartwheeling twins and spent the day moving into the apartment above Hillview Vet. The first thing Mom did in our new temporary home was hang the *mezuzah* that used to be on the frame of the front door of our forever home. The first thing I did was put my stuffed platypus, Pepper, on my bed. Dad got him for me one weekend when we ran to Harvey's General Store to get the things on Mom's to-do list. The platypus was sitting on a shelf by himself.

Dad said we couldn't leave him behind. So we bought him and brought him home.

The next thing I did in my new temporary home was let Pickle choose the color to paint our shared bedroom. She picked light purple like the lilacs at our forever home.

"We came here because Mom started working at All for You—it's a national, grassroots women's rights organization in town." I follow Logan into the kitchen. "She said the change would be good. Moving out of the city would be good." She pauses. "I guess, but Chicago still has the best pizza." There are photos covering the wall on the right of her with her mom and dad. Most are from when Logan was little. They're all smiling.

We each grab a slice of the now-cold deep-dish pizza with extra cheese, Logan pours us tall glasses of pink lemonade, and we head to her room. There's a big oval mirror on the far wall and four different pairs of glasses sitting on top of the dresser. The walls are a cool ice blue.

"I like it in here because it's the same color as my bedroom when we lived in Chicago," Logan says, swapping out her black-rimmed glasses for a pair of speckled ones.

I wonder if Prisha's new room is pale yellow.

Then, while we're sitting there, between bites of pizza, Logan grabs long, metal tongs and picks up a thawed frozen rat to give to Snow White like it's not scary or gross.

My eyes widen.

"Want to try feeding her?" Logan asks.

"Um, no thanks," I say, hoping I don't sound as scared as I feel. Because even though I've seen snakes at Hillview Vet, I've never actually fed one.

Logan dangles the dead rodent by the tail in front of her pet snake. "You know, she's actually really shy," Logan says as Snow White bites the rat and rolls quickly around to coil it.

I nod, thankful that guinea pigs eat fruits and vegetables.

"When we first got her, my dad was worried she'd eat his crickets. But then was relieved when he saw the frozen dead rats," Logan says, laughing. "What does your dad do?"

"He's in the Peace Corps."

"My mom had a friend who did that. It's totally cool."

I nod as if each night before I fall asleep, I don't cross my fingers and wish he'd come home.

Logan eats a cricket and then offers me one. I hesitate, but don't want her to think I'm scared to do this, too, so I pop it in my mouth. It's crunchy and not as gross as I was sure it would be. But still not as good as pizza.

"Is it weird that he's away?" she asks.

I take a giant gulp of lemonade and nod. My words are stuck behind cricket and a mound of missing.

She puts her hand on mine. "I get it. I mean, my mom's not away, but she works so much that sometimes it feels that way," Logan says, eating a second cricket.

Then she leans in close. "Guess what! I did it."

"Did what?" I look around hoping for a clue. But all I see on the ice blue walls are the mirror, two posters of Ruth Bader Ginsburg, and lots of photos of Snow White.

"I applied to be Dear Student," she says, picking up a bottle of bright purple nail polish.

I bite my lip.

"Isn't that supposed to be a secret?"

As soon as the words fly out of my mouth, I know by the look on Logan's face they were the exact wrong thing to say. I cough. "I just mean from other people. Not me."

Her hurt look fades.

"Plus, I think you'd be supergood at it."

She smiles.

"You should have applied," Logan says. "I bet you'd

give good advice. Like how to wash down a crunchy cricket." She laughs.

On the outside I laugh with Logan. But on the inside, I feel hot and nauseous and am having trouble breathing like a normal person.

Should I have told her that I changed my mind? That I applied even though that day in the cafeteria I shook my head like there was no way I'd ever apply?

Is not telling the same as lying?

My worries stick and I wonder if I just ruined everything.

11

Big Ball of Worries

I try to sleep. But it's not happening. Maybe I should have told Logan. Maybe it wouldn't have been weird. But I didn't. So now it *is* weird. And the worries won't stop spinning in my brain.

I look over at Pickle, who's curled in a ball, snoring. I open the small wooden box that sits on the table between our two beds and take out the postcards from Dad. I read them all, then try to sleep again. My dreams fill with colorful markets and classrooms of kids halfway around the world eating cheese eggs and asking advice from Dear Student.

At some point when the sky becomes that almost-morning color, I email Prisha.

Hi, Prisha!

I think I made a ginormous mistake and my worried feelings are like spilled paint spreading everywhere : (

I tell her about Logan and applying to Dear Student and keeping it a secret. Ask her about her new school. Then fill her in on Hillview Middle.

There are french fries at lunch. Which is a very good thing. There's a lot more homework. Which is not a very good thing. And I still haven't found Fearless Fred. Help!

I miss you. Huge!

xoxo

A

It's still nighttime there, so I know I won't hear back until later. I hit Send, and when the sky turns the actual color of morning, I get out of bed. I need to find Mom. I don't want to talk, but I do want permission to walk Bear. My worries need air. And I already know Malcolm is at work because I see his silver Honda with the dent on the bumper in the parking lot.

I hide the prickly feeling climbing across my skin and smile like I'm not worried at all. In ten minutes, Bear and I are heading to King's Beach. When we get there, I unhook him and he sprints into the ocean. I kick off my sneakers and walk along the sand. The white foamy waves roll over my bare toes. A seagull hops alongside me as the misty, salty air drapes across my goosebumps. I wonder if he can sense when someone's worried.

"So, what do you think?" I ask my bird buddy. "Did I make a mistake?"

He looks at me with his black button eyes, then caws loudly.

"You're right. Logan's not going to care."

Another caw.

"And it's supposed to be a secret anyway."

The seagull flies away and dives into the ocean.

"It doesn't even really matter because there's no way I'm going to get picked," I say, laughing at my feathered friend who now has a crab dangling from its beak. I walk and think and walk and think. Yep. The bird's right. Logan won't be mad. If she ever finds out. Which she won't. I spy a clamshell and wonder how big the clam was that used to live in there.

I scoop up the perfectly white, ridged shell and tuck it into my backpack. It's beautiful. When I look up, I recognize the person walking toward me.

It's Cooper with a big fluffy dog.

At this moment, I'm happy I'm not wearing my favorite soft mustard-stained sweatshirt.

"Hola," he says as his dog licks the saltwater off my toes. "This is Mr. Magoo." He smiles.

I kneel and rub behind Mr. Magoo's ears, thinking of something to say. I settle on "He's supercute," hoping that sounds normal. Then Cooper tosses a yellow tennis ball in the water and his dog sprints after it.

The waves crest and fall and Cooper points to Mr. Magoo, who's now swimming in circles with the ball in his mouth, and laughs. "He loves high tide."

"How old is he?" I say, staring at Bear, who's trying to dig up a hermit crab.

Cooper shrugs. "Don't know. I found him living on the street near our apartment. He kept coming around, dirty and hungry and skinny. No one claimed him, so we took him in."

"He's lucky you found him." After the hurricane in the Carolinas last year, my mom said so many dogs and cats and birds and lizards and turtles got separated from their families.

"I'm lucky he found me." He whistles and Mr. Magoo

sprints toward him. "He's the only good thing about moving to this place."

Oh.

Mr. Magoo comes over and starts digging with Bear. I step left to avoid the flying sand.

The silence feels awkward.

Say something. My brain searches for words that don't fall squarely in the weird-things-kids-don't-say category.

But then Cooper asks, "How's the iguana?"

"Better," I say, poking my toes into the sand.

"Good." He tosses the tennis ball back into the water. "Hey, sorry I bolted the other day. Just had to get to school. First day. You know."

I nod. "Why, um, didn't you just say you weren't some random tourist?" I cross my fingers behind my back and pray that doesn't sound like I think he owes me some sort of explanation.

He shrugs. "Didn't think that really mattered. Just thought you guys would be mad that I had to bail before we knew the iguana was okay. I don't know." He shoves his hands into his pockets. "I'm not the best at that stuff."

I look up at Cooper and I want to tell him that I'm not good at that stuff either, but the words stick.

Bear drops a clump of wet seaweed at my feet. "No one's mad," I say.

More awkward silence.

I bite my lip, wishing for Cooper to say something else. But he doesn't. The silence twists, pulling at me to fill it. Finally I say, "Would have told you about Superman at school. But didn't see you at, um, lunch." I stare at the waves rolling onto the sand.

"I kind of hate cafeterias. Too noisy. Too many people."

"Oh. I thought that was just me."

We laugh. Which feels nice. And easy. And not filled with worries.

My phone buzzes. It's Mom. She wants me to come home so we can go back-to-school shopping. Even though we're already back.

Mr. Magoo shakes his wet fur. I look at Cooper, who's now covered with salty ocean water.

"I've got to head home." I pat Mr. Magoo.

"Cool," he says, pulling down his Wizards cap. "I'll be in the science lab on Monday during lunch. If you want to ditch the whole cafeteria thing. Ms. Murphy said I could eat there anytime."

"Who's Ms. Murphy?"

"My biology teacher."

I smile. "See you there."

12

A Lot of Dead Things

"I really don't need anything but my cape," Pickle says as she gets into the truck. Most kids picked up school supplies and clothes and other stuff they needed before school started, but Mom was working and Dad was somewhere near the equator.

"Not sure naked in a cape is the best way to go through kindergarten," I tell her.

She puts her little hands on her hips. "I didn't mean I'd *just* wear my cape."

It takes us two hours too long to get everything. Mostly because Pickle can't decide between a yellow notebook with a happy sun or a purple one with a tree. Ultimately, she chooses purple to match the polish Logan painted on my nails. And while she's deciding, I get to pick out a new phone from the row of discounted ones. Which should make me one hundred percent happy, except Mom said I needed it because she's relying on me more. And she's relying on me more because Dad left. And that's the part that makes me less than one hundred percent happy.

We put Pickle's markers, colored pencils, and notebook, along with my new penguin shirt, five folders, and pack of mechanical pencils, in the back of the truck. I hold on to my phone. Then we pile in and Mom puts on her Best of the '80s playlist, which she listens to when she's missing Dad the most. I take in a big breath of Bon Jovi because I know what's coming.

Mom leans back and hands us a new postcard from Dad.

Hello from Ecuador!

I spent the day reading to the kids in the school. It feels like I can really make a difference here. I'm thinking of you both and sending love as you start the new school year. Remember, be fearless and seize the day.

Your Loving Dad

Pickle starts to cry. I hold my little sister's hand. "Don't worry. You're already fearless!"

She wipes her cheeks and rests her head of curls on my shoulder. It smells like strawberry.

"I don't get why he sends these." I draw a sad face in the fog on the truck's window.

"He misses you," Mom says.

"Then he should come home."

Mom spins around. "I know this is hard. It's difficult for all of us." She pauses. "But Dad's doing something he felt he had to do. He signed up right after he turned the age Papa Fred was when he died. It took a lot of courage to make that decision."

"Not sure leaving is courageous," I say, erasing my window drawing with my palm.

She doesn't say anything. Then, "I love you girls." She turns back around as "Livin' on a Prayer" echoes through the car.

When we get to Hillview Vet, Malcolm comes over to us. "Dr. Blake, you got another gift."

I cringe. Over the years, Mom's gotten a lot of dead things for presents. Ms. Bogart brought her a dead raccoon she found during a walk with her dog down by the river. It's now taxidermied and in the back hall near Exam Room 2. The Greens gave her a dead crayfish they found at the beach. She's also received the skeletons of a skunk and a duck.

"Should we open it?" Malcolm asks.

Mom looks at me.

"Definitely," I say, eyeing the box, still holding my little sister's hand.

The four of us slowly peel back the silver wrapping paper and the large bow. Turns out the present is from Joshua Gregory as a thank-you for taking good care of Hashtag, his very sick, very old hamster.

Mom lifts the gift from the paper. It's a long sliver of bones from some kind of dead snake.

"Maybe one day you'll get flowers," Malcolm says, laughing.

Mom smiles, then checks on Sugar the tarantula, who hasn't been eating her crickets.

I read a new email from Prisha.

A,

Miss you, girlfriend! You did nothing wrong. You're allowed to apply and not say anything. That's part of the job. So stop worrying.

Totally get what you mean about too much

homework. I hate geometry. When will I ever need to know anything about a rhombus in real life?

I'm auditioning for the school play, Hairspray. Wish me luck! Remember that time we sang all the songs in our pajamas and used toilet paper rolls as our mics?

XO,

Prisha

I send her a quick update back.

Hi Prisha,

Good luck with the tryouts. You'll be great! You're a star!

And I promise, I'll try to stop worrying. Would be easier if we were together eating your nani's amazing pea and potato samosas! Miss those. And miss you.

Guess what? I got a phone. So now we can text!

xoxo

A

I immediately text Prisha. She got a phone last year. And when my phone pings, I think it's her texting back, but it's Dad: *Mom sent me your #. Thinking of you! Love you.*

I don't do anything for a moment. Not sure what I want to say. Part of me wants to tell him I applied, but the other part worries that if I don't get it, he'll be disappointed in me. Again.

Instead I text: *Got a great idea. Come home for my and Pickle's birthdays! Then we won't have to text* 🙂

Next ping I think is Dad, but it's Prisha—she texts a heart, a happy face, and a whale emoji. I'm not sure why the whale, but I reply with a thumbs-up.

Then I text Logan. Like normal. Like I did nothing wrong.

Logan texts back: *Yay, you got a phone! Perfect timing. Been dying to talk. Do you think I'll get the Dear Student thing? I hope so*

My worries are back.

13

Frozen Rat

Logan invites me over on Sunday. When I get there, she's feeding Snow White a thawed frozen rat. Not sure I'll ever get used to that. We watch her ball python swallow her lunch for a while and then it's our turn. Not for frozen rodents, but for lunch. Logan's made two sandwiches. Ham and Swiss, and tuna. I take the tuna, then she hands me half her ham and Swiss.

"Um, no thanks. I'm good with the tuna. Especially with chips crunched in." I take a handful and put them in the middle of my sandwich, hoping that's not weird because it's hands-down the best way to eat tuna.

"I know, but we can swap," she says, putting half of her sandwich on my plate.

I look at it and am not sure what I'm supposed to do. She's staring at me and my tuna.

I don't even like ham.

She smiles.

But I do like having a friend who wants to share.

I hand her half of my tuna-potato-chip masterpiece as I think of ways to subtly not eat my ham sandwich.

"Thanks," she says, stealing a look at herself in the mirror. "Maybe next time we can meet at your house. Where do you live?"

My throat feels like sandpaper. I sip my lemonade. "Above Hillview Vet. In an apartment."

She nods. "Cool."

"It's temporary. You know, just until my dad comes back."

"Yeah. I get it." She takes a bite of her ham sandwich and then the tuna and then the ham again. "How long is temporary?"

I look down to hide the tears that might leak out. "Um, the whole thing is supposed to be two years, plus, like, three months for training in the beginning."

"Wow. That's a long time. Feels kind of not really temporary."

My insides crumble.

"No. He's definitely coming back," I say too quickly. "He's actually coming home soon for a visit." I know I just invited him and he hasn't said yes yet, but I need to believe this is true.

"Maybe we can get him to try a cricket." She tosses her empty paper plate in the garbage and turns around quickly. "I just thought of the best idea."

I cross my fingers behind my back and hope this isn't about my dad.

"Let's wear matching shirts tomorrow."

I exhale. But then remember what's in my closet. "I'm pretty sure we don't own matching anything."

"I didn't mean identical shirts. That's like what fourth graders do."

I never did that in fourth grade.

"We should wear ones that go together and are about the same thing. Like girl power or Earth Day or ninjas or animals."

I look down at my Happy Manatee shirt. "I have a new penguin tee or one with a white, black, and gray wolf on the front that says MISSION WOLF across the back."

"What's that?"

"A wolf sanctuary. I volunteered there for a week last summer."

With Prisha.

"Weren't you scared? I mean, the wolves could have totally eaten you," Logan says.

"Not really. I helped feed and take care of them. They were beautiful. Especially Angel. She had these see-through crystal-blue eyes."

"I don't have a wolf shirt, but I have one with elephants on it. The baby elephant's trunk is up, which is good luck."

So now I know when I walk back into Hillview Middle School for my first full week of sixth grade tomorrow, I'll be wearing matching T-shirts with my new friend.

14

Prickly Nerves

When I step into the kitchen before school on Monday, Pickle's at the table wrapped in her lime-green cape with a book in her lap, not eating her waffles.

"It's not working," she says.

"What's not working?" I ask, sitting down next to her.

"My cape. It's broken. I think all the superpowers leaked out when Mom washed it."

I touch the tips of Pickle's cape. "Nope, they're still there. I can feel them." I slide a waffle onto my plate with a heaping spoonful of blueberries and whipped cream.

My little sister smiles. "Will you read to me?" she asks.

I nod.

Pickle moves onto my lap and we read *Drawn Together,* a book with few words and lots of heart. That's what Dad used to say every time he read it aloud.

When we're done with the story, we share my waffle and read it again. And again. And again.

"Most of the kids in kindergarten know how to read," Pickle says. Her lips twist. "Except me."

"That's okay. You're a great swimmer and a fast runner."

"Just like Dad. He's superfast," she says, smiling.

I nod. It's true. But my words are lodged behind lots of missing and a sprinkling of mad. When this whole leaving thing happened, I got it. Sort of. I honestly thought he'd be gone for a month at most and then come back because he missed us too much. But it's been a little over a year and he's still not home.

Is Logan right? Does temporary really mean forever?

He only gets time off after, like, a year. Dad says it's okay because he made a commitment. And they need him.

But *I* need him.

Why doesn't that count? Why isn't that enough? Why am I not enough?

Pickle taps my arm. "Do you think I'll ever learn to read?"

"Yes," I say, tucking away my mad and sad. Because

right now my little sister needs me. And I never want her to think that she's not enough.

I read the book one more time. Hug her tight. Then text Logan.

We meet at the corner of Alpine and Baron Drive and walk to school together with our sort-of matching shirts. While we walk, I count steps between neighborhood pets. There are 152 steps between Blue the beagle and Cali, the Murphys' Maine coon who's striped like a tiger.

"Did you decide what you're going to say for Baker's get-to-know-you thing?" Logan asks.

This took me a really long time last night. First, I shot a video of me making whoopie pies. But when I played it back, it made me think of Dad in the sad-missing kind of way. And I'm definitely not sharing that. I tried drawing my answers, but quickly realized I'm still a terrible artist. So I moved on to writing. I filled it in. Deleted it. Filled it in again.

I think I know what I'm going to share, but don't want to tell Logan yet. So I just nod. "What about you?"

"For the 'something about yourself' part, I'm going to share how I can stand on my hands for eighty-six seconds."

I give her a thumbs-up.

Then right there on the Hunts' front lawn, she drops

ckpack and does a handstand. Just like that. No
s that it's weird or embarrassing.

ount," she says to me, now upside-down.

I count and decide there's no way I'm talking about my absent dad, my temporary home, or our last family trip to Sea World.

She puts her feet back on the ground. "How long?"

"Sixty-three seconds," I say.

"With some added because you started late."

There are another forty-seven steps to get to Melon the long-haired mutt and Barney the bunny. After that, I don't see another pet until I spy the dog in front of the school with Reilly Rain.

I wait until Logan stops talking about her handstand. I inhale my brave and start to cough.

Logan turns to me. "You okay?"

I nod.

This is it. Just ask.

Last night I decided to invite Logan to my cupcake birthday celebration with Pickle. I considered also asking Cooper, but thought that might be weird since the party isn't really a party. And he's a friend, but also a guy. So Prisha and I agreed that Logan was the exact right new friend to ask.

I cross my fingers behind my back. Out of sight. And say in a voice covered with prickly nerves, "So, um, I wanted to know if you maybe wanted to come for cupcakes on Sunday." I pause. "For, um, my birthday."

"Of course! I love parties!"

I'm not sure cupcakes with my five-year-old sister, her friends, some animals, and my mom at Hillview Vet qualifies as a party.

15

Hairy Caterpillars

When we get to Room 707, Mr. Baker's outside greeting everyone. His jolly voice echoes down the hall. "Hellooooo!" he says to the kid with the baseball cap on backwards. "It's going to be a wonderful day!" he says to the girl with the head full of beautiful braids. And as we turn in to the room, he says, "Great morning!" like he's going to burst into song.

Logan rolls her eyes. But it makes me happy.

Mr. Baker kicks off the get-to-know-you activity by having his answers to the five questions already written on the board when we walk in.

1. SOMETHING ABOUT MYSELF: I'm scared of hairy caterpillars.
2. SOMETHING ABOUT MY FAMILY OR NEIGHBORHOOD: I live in an apartment six blocks from school with my two-year-old mutt named Baxter who drinks out of the toilet.
3. SOMETHING I LOVE TO DO: Read a whole book in one big gulp.
4. SOMETHING I HATE TO DO: Stop reading in the middle of a book.
5. SOMETHING I WANT TO LEARN: How not to be afraid of hairy caterpillars.

Then he goes around the room. Reggie with the long blond hair is up first. He tells us his face blows up like a balloon if he eats shrimp.

My body stiffens. I count. I'm four away. I barely hear when Reilly Rain tells the class about Maisy, her honey-colored golden retriever, who is a service dog.

Sophie's next.

My brain feels like fog.

She shows a video of her many attempts to do a cartwheel with her eyes closed.

Now it's Logan's turn. She stands and her smile

stretches across her face. She has no hives or red blotches on her neck. I try to focus and nod when she shares about her handstand, which she promises to show everyone tomorrow before school on the front lawn. Next, she holds up a photo of Snow White, and then reads a newspaper article about the time in Chicago when she raised money for a family in her neighborhood whose house was damaged by fire. She takes out the printed version so we can see the photo of a younger Logan smiling.

She's almost done. A bead of sweat trickles down my neck.

"The one thing I hate doing is"—she pauses and glances at the papers on her desk—"stuff alone. You know, when your mom's busy changing the world, that can happen sometimes."

That makes me feel a tug sad.

"Thank you, Logan," Mr. Baker says, "Okay, Autumn, you're up."

I don't stand. Don't look at all the eyes staring back at me. I sit on my shaking hands, look at my paper, and hope the heat spreading across my face isn't visible. Then, in a low whisper, I say, "I love working at Hillview Vet and taking care of the different kinds of animals."

"Autumn, please speak a little louder so we can all hear you," Mr. Baker says.

I inhale in a big breath of nerves and raise my voice.

A little. "I have a pet guinea pig named Spud. I like writing and hate dancing. And I want to learn more about iguanas and snakes."

I wipe my sweaty palms on my jeans and exhale.

I did it.

I shared.

After we go around the room, I know that Lilac Shirt's name is Evie and she's a twin, Jules sometimes sneezes fifteen times after eating a big chicken dinner, and Everett also hates dancing. Which makes me feel better about sharing. It was between that and brussels sprouts. And nobody else said anything about hating brussels sprouts.

The rest of the morning is filled with pre-algebra and history. Eventually, I head to the cafeteria, which is jammed with a giant pod of sixth graders. I need to find a way to get a large container of french fries out of the cafeteria and into the science lab to meet Cooper.

While I'm plotting my strategy, Logan links her arm in mine and tries to shepherd me toward a table.

"I, um, need to get something from the science lab for my homework, so I'm just going to eat quickly while I'm there."

That is the truth. Just not all of the truth. The rest of my words knot behind the tangled feelings I get navigating two friends.

"What is it with you and the cafeteria?" she asks.

I say nothing because the answer to that *is* embarrassing.

"I promise to share my fries." She holds up the basket of fries she already has in her hand.

I smile. "Thanks. But I'm going to eat in the science lab. Want to come?"

She shakes her head. "I try to avoid quiet, empty places." She laughs.

"Well, it's not totally empty. There's this kid Cooper who hangs out there."

There. All of the truth.

She points to the crowded, loud cafeteria. "I like it here." She pushes up her glasses and leans in close. "I really just wanted to talk about your party. It's going to be awesome. I can't wait to meet all your other friends."

My other friends?

"It's small. You know, not a big thing," I say.

"I totally get it." She winks. "You're at a new school with new friends. You can't invite everyone." She nods toward Evie, Jules, Maya, and Reilly, who are waving her over to the table. "I mean, you have to include your friends from your old elementary school, too."

Uh-oh.

I try to turn on my mind-to-mind thing. That's what Prisha and I call it when we read each other's thoughts.

"Maybe you, me, and your other friends can hang out after the party," Logan says.

But it's not working.

My brain twists and bends. How am I going to tell Logan the party isn't really a party?

So, Logan, about my birthday. Think a few five-year-olds, a bunch of odd animals, cupcakes, and, um, you.

Or:

Logan, what's better than five-year-olds, pets, and cupcakes? Nothing, am I right?

I can't find the right words.

Maybe they don't exist.

16

Gone

When I get to the science lab, I'm worry-sweating. I don't know how this birthday thing got so messed up.

"Hey." It's Cooper, wearing the same tan shirt and Washington Wizards cap he had on when I saw him at the beach.

Okay, deep breath. Don't be weird.

I slide my backpack off in a way that I hope looks normal, but is really wiping the sweat trickling down my neck.

I grab a seat across from Cooper and get a whiff of his peanut butter sandwich.

We talk about Superman and how I think he might be lonely. And then Cooper wants to know what it's like living above Hillview Vet.

"I get to visit the animals all the time. And because we live next door to my favorite ice cream place, our apartment always smells like homemade waffle cones." I focus on the good stuff and leave out the part about it not feeling like home.

I watch him swig his milk and am happy I brought water. I don't like drinking anything from a carton. The lip always gets soggy before I get to the bottom.

Then he asks, "Does your dad work there too?"

I feel the heat spread across my face and pray the bad lighting hides the hives I know are popping up on my neck.

"No. He's in Ecuador, working for the Peace Corps."

"What's that?" he asks.

"An organization that sends volunteers all over the world to do lots of different things. Some help build homes or help with farming or environmental kind of stuff."

Cooper shoves half his sandwich in his mouth.

"My dad's in a school over there working with some of the local teachers."

"That's cool," he says. "You're lucky."

I nod like that's exactly how I feel. Then wonder how my dad being thousands of miles away in another country is lucky.

"Mine's gone too. Not like doing something good in the world, like yours. Just gone gone. He took off after I was born."

"Sorry," I say, feeling a squeeze of guilt. Maybe it's not so bad that my dad's thousands of miles away in another country.

"My mom makes up for it. She's pretty cool. I mean, she let me keep Mr. Magoo."

I smile and decide I like it here surrounded by microscopes, a life-size skeleton Cooper named Mr. Bean, and a row of mason jars filled with liquids and some random stuff.

The bell rings. Lunch is over.

I spend the rest of the school day trying to find Logan to clear up the birthday misunderstanding, but I don't see her until the club fair starts. And by that time my mind's spinning and my heart's pounding. Thankfully, my panic mode is tucked inside. Logan doesn't notice as we walk to the tables lining the hall with Evie and Jules following close behind. At the Chess Club table, there are two kids in the middle of a match. The Dance Club is blaring country music. I like the song, but already know that club isn't right for me. I look around and know I need to find something if I ever want my dad to come home. No word yet on Dear Student, and Dad sent me another text earlier today about my just one thing. I try to channel Fearless Fred, but it's not working.

Logan's talking to everyone, always knowing the right thing to say. It's like watching the bakers on *The Great British Baking Show* masterfully create a Victorian cake shaped like a tennis court.

"Autumn, what about the Fashion Club?" Logan asks, pulling me to the table covered in fun hats, hoop earrings, and lots of scarves. "We could get matching hats." She picks up a midnight-black fedora and pulls it over her blond hair. "I love it," she says, popping a navy one onto my head.

"You look so cute." She hands me the small mirror that's on the table and says, "We so have to join this club."

I look in the mirror and wonder if this is what brave looks like. Then my head starts to itch and I decide it's not. But I don't want to say no, so I just say, "Maybe."

An older boy in a green beret says, "You guys should sign up. We make cool stuff for each other." He points to the girl behind the booth who is wearing a leopard-print scarf. "And sell some of it to raise money for the residents at the Ridge Senior Home."

Logan writes her name on the sign-up sheet, and the

boy in the beret who seems to be in charge hands me the paper.

"I'm going to think about it," I say, silently promising to bring Spud to visit the seniors so long as that's a thing guinea pigs are allowed to do.

I'm ready with my promised-my-mom-I'd-work excuse if Logan asks why I didn't sign up, but she doesn't ask. She's already talking to the Spanish Club people, the Popcorn and Movie Club people, the Power in Numbers Math Club people. Then she skips over to the table with the sign SOCIAL JUSTICE—YOUR VOICE MATTERS.

"This is the one, Autumn!" Logan rushes up to the eighth grader behind the table who introduces herself as the club president, Zahara Jones.

As Zahara gushes about the club, her dangly earrings sparkle. "We're already planning our first event. You guys should totally come. It's a letter-writing campaign to advocate that girls around the globe have access to education."

"I'm in!" Logan says, scribbling her name, email, and phone number on the paper and handing it to Zahara.

"Wait, are you related to JoJo Bellingham?" Zahara asks.

Logan's smile turns up. "Yep, that's my mom."

"I saw that clip of her talking to the press after winning that case against that tech company for equal pay. You know, the one where the head of the company she sued walked by and rolled his eyes. Wow! What a jerk. The whole thing totally went viral. She's amazing." Zahara calls to the other club members. "Hey, this girl's mom is JoJo Bellingham," she says, pointing to Logan. "Your mom's, like, famous."

"Thanks." Logan smiles.

"We'll be in touch with the information for the next meeting. Maybe you could get your mom to stop by," Zahara says.

"Sure. I'll ask her," Logan says.

I see Logan smile, but it doesn't look like a real one.

"You okay?" I ask as we make our way to the end of the hall.

She nods. "It happens all the time. The most exciting thing about me is my mom."

My heart dips.

"I think you're more exciting than your mom." I pause. "No offense to your mom."

Logan smiles a real smile. "Thanks."

I'm about to tell her about the party when I spy Cooper at the *Express* table. He waves. I wave back, and by the time I turn around, Logan's moved on to the Book

Club and Geared-Up Engineering Club. She puts her name down for each and we head out the front door of the school.

"How are you going to do all those clubs you signed up for *and* Dear Student?" I ask.

"I don't know if I'm even going to get the advice column thing. But I'm totally doing the club with Zahara. I mean, I know she's all into my mom being famous. But she's still cool." She pops a sour lemon candy into her mouth and hands me one. "What about you? Which ones are you going to do?" she asks.

That's when I realize my new friend didn't even notice that I hadn't put my name down on a single sign-up sheet.

17

Close Enough

I get up extra early and look in the mirror. Today's the day Mr. Baker picks the new secret voice of Dear Student. I weave in my orange ribbon just how Prisha showed me. I want to look fearless. Even if my stomach's swarming with bees.

"Oooh, I like your twisty hair," Pickle says, walking over to my side of the room.

"Thanks."

"Will you twist mine?" She points to her uncombed head of wild curls that's just like Mom's. I got Dad's brown wavy hair. Which I love. And his big earlobes. Which I love less.

"Sure," I say. I grab two shiny barrettes and brush and twist my little sister's hair. Her tiny fingers rest on my knee.

She peeks in the mirror. "Can I have a ribbon like yours?"

I run my hand along the orange ribbon Prisha gave me. I don't want to cut the thing that connects me to Prisha. But I do want my sister to feel connected to something. Or someone. And since Dad left and Mom's working all the time, that someone is me.

I pull out my ribbon, cut it into two pieces, and weave one into my twist and the other into Pickle's until we match.

"Now we're twins!" The sister part of me is happy. The daughter part is mad. I shouldn't have to be her person because our person is halfway around the world seizing the day.

Then she hops onto my bed. "Can you read this with me?" Pickle hands me a postcard from Dad.

I read Dad's words from somewhere on the other side of the world.

Hello, sunshine!

I'm thinking of you. I just made whoopie pies for my class. They loved them.

And next I'm on the lookout for a tapir.
Wow! So much world to see.
Remember to seize the day!

Your Loving Dad

"At least we'll see him soon," she says.

My breath catches in the back of my throat. I haven't heard back from him since I asked him to come home for our birthdays. I've been thinking that maybe he is going to surprise us. But maybe I'm wrong. Maybe he already told Pickle that he's coming back. "What do you mean, we'll see him soon?"

"It's our birthdays. He wouldn't miss them again," she says. "Also, I've been wishing for this every night before I go to sleep."

And I invited him.

My brain flickers with maybes as Pickle skips out of my room.

I grab my laptop. I emailed my Kiko story to Mr. Baker last night. It was part of our homework. But before putting my laptop in my backpack, I look over what I wrote one more time.

Kiko slipped back home. The smells of the cinnamon reeds she got for her room filled in around her. She removed her shadow of invisibility and gave Apollo a cricket. Then she sat on her bed. "Why would someone do that? Why would someone write those awful things?" she said. "I don't understand humans, Apollo. My heart feels heavy." She wished her powers included the ability to change minds.

When she got to the temple, Kiko lowered her invisible body into a velvet-lined seat. She was surrounded by angry words. The stained-glass windows were splashed with hate. No one was around. But she stayed hidden as she painted over the graffiti. She turned the ugly messages into a beautiful mural of hands holding onto each other. Then slipped back into the night.

It's so much easier to find the words when they aren't for me. When I don't have to say them out loud.

I close my computer and head to school. Time to find out if I'm the next Dear Student.

Almost Normal

"Your hair looks really cute," Logan says when she sees me in English.

I run my fingers along my smaller orange ribbon.

"We should totally wear our hair like that when we go to the dance on Friday," she says.

I swallow hard.

I'm terrified to go to this dance.

But more terrified to bail on my new best friend.

"Everyone online says that each year, Baker chooses the new Dear Student in the morning," she whispers. "I so want to get this!"

"Good luck," I say, hoping it's okay to wish her luck and still want Baker to pick me.

Mr. Baker steps to the front of the classroom and waves two fingers in the air, the sign for us to stop talking. He clears his throat. "Whenever you're ready, Autumn."

Heat swarms my face. I don't want to read my story. Not now. My hands shake. I want to know who he picked for Dear Student. It's weird how the closer it gets, the more I want it. The more I know this should be my one thing. I cough and take a sip from my water bottle, hoping if I take too long, Mr. Baker will skip me.

But he doesn't. He waits for me to finish drinking and smiles my way. I pray my voice doesn't crack. I read more of my story about Kiko and Apollo and the hate and the beautiful mural. My voice is low as I share how love can turn even the ugliest words into something beautiful. When I'm done, Reilly and Destiny clap loudly.

I exhale.

"Great job, Autumn," Mr. Baker says.

Relief washes over me.

Richie raises his hand. "Why does Kiko use her invisibility powers to do something nice? I mean, if I did all that good stuff, I'd want people to know it was me."

I don't want to answer. I want Mr. Baker to move on. But he doesn't. He looks my way. Waits for me to respond. My insides dip. "I, um, thought that, um." I stare at my paper, praying the next words that come out of my mouth aren't dumb. "Kiko's shy. She feels safer doing stuff when no one can see her."

I stop talking, hoping I said enough.

Time stalls.

My nerves bleed and stretch.

I wait for something.

Mr. Baker nods. "Like Wonder Woman or Spider-man. Think how many of today's superheroes hide in plain sight even though they're protecting and helping others."

I breathe out.

"There are totally times when I want to do something nice, but am too nervous to just do it," Destiny says.

"Yeah, like last year, this guy anonymously bought new sneakers for all the kids at the Pine Forest Family Shelter. His story totally went viral even though no one ever knew who the guy actually was," Maya says.

It's Evie's turn. She reads a poem about feeling like half a grapefruit. And Everett reads a story about zombies and werewolves taking over the school dance. I smile, remembering that he hates dancing.

Most of the school day is almost normal except for the whispering and wondering about who was picked to be Dear Student. Logan said Mr. Baker makes his choice in the morning. So by midday, all I know is that it wasn't me. Disappointment spreads across my brain as I grab my history homework, which has sunk to the bottom of my locker.

Maybe I'll never find Fearless Fred. Or my just-one-thing.

Maybe I'll never make my dad proud.

Maybe temporary really is forever.

"Who do you think got it?" Jules asks. Her locker's next to mine.

I shrug.

"Was it you?" she asks, smiling.

I smile back as my insides twist.

"She didn't even apply," Logan says, walking up to us.

I don't bother correcting her, because it doesn't matter now anyway. I didn't get it.

"Maybe it's that kid Everett," Jules says. "He seemed way happy this afternoon for like no reason at all."

"Maybe Baker's picking an eighth grader this year. I saw Lucinda talking to him before second period, and I heard she doesn't even have him as a teacher," Logan says, offering us some of her sour lemon candies.

"Oooh, maybe," Jules says, taking two candies and giving us a wave. "Gotta run. I need help with integers and my math teacher said she'd meet me before class."

I see Logan talking to Zahara from the Your Voice

Matters Club. Then Cooper walks over to my locker. Which feels surprising and awkward and kind of nice.

"Hey. I was thinking. Maybe we should try to find Superman's owner," Cooper says, shoving his hands into his pockets.

"Do you know iguanas have a third eye right in the middle of their foreheads? It helps protect them from predators."

Cooper smiles. "Cool." He pulls down his Wizards cap. "I know Malcolm posted stuff on the Hillview Vet site. But maybe we could do something more. Like make posters or a video."

"We could shoot a video with Superman," I say. "Like a *Have You Seen Me?* type of thing," I add, remembering this one video I saw on YouTube for a missing parrot named Radio.

"And we—"

Before he can finish, Logan darts over to us. "I'm so excited!"

She doesn't pause for me to ask why or to introduce her to Cooper. She just dives in. "Zahara told me the first meeting for the Your Voice Matters Club is Saturday. And we'll be planning a letter-writing campaign. And—"

"This Saturday?" I ask.

My birthday.

Logan nods. "Wait for it. The best part. She asked if I'd help organize." She continues without taking a breath. "Of course I said yes! And, my first job is to ask my mom to stop by the meeting."

At this moment, I hope our mind-to-mind thing is shut off.

"What time on Saturday?" I ask.

"Noon. I can't wait. It's going to be the Best. Day. Ever! I think I'm going to bring donuts. Or no, maybe brownies."

I say nothing, hoping she can't see the bricks of disappointment filling my insides.

She freezes and stares at me. "I totally forgot."

Which doesn't make me feel any better.

"Forgot what?" Cooper asks.

"Nothing," I say, as I speed-walk away from my embarrassment and head straight to my next class.

I spend the next two hours trying to avoid Logan, but she finds me at the end of the day. "Look, I'm really sorry about your party," she says.

"It's no big deal," I tell her, shutting off the part of my brain that says I'm lying. The part that wishes I really didn't care.

19

I'd Rather Eat Crickets

"You're the best! I totally wouldn't go if Zahara hadn't asked me to organize it," she says. "But we can celebrate your birthday at the dance."

I'd rather eat crickets.

"It'll be fun. I promise," she adds, giving me a hug.

I nod like that's the best idea.

Like I don't hate to dance.

Like I'm not terrified to go.

I say goodbye to Logan and head down the empty hall. I spy Mr. Baker coming out of the teachers' lounge and wave.

"This is a happy accident," Mr. Baker says, wearing

his BOOKS SAVE THE WORLD T-shirt. "I was just coming to look for you."

"Why?" I ask. My nerves ricochet across my chest as I wonder how many things can go wrong in one day.

"I need to talk to you a minute."

As I follow him down the hall to his empty classroom, my brain catalogs all the reasons I could be in trouble. Was the writing I turned in too short? Did I miss an assignment? Does he hate iguanas?

Mr. Baker grabs a king-size bag of sour cream and onion chips from his desk drawer and offers me some.

That's a good sign. No one who's supermad would offer me chips.

"You're a good writer," he says.

Another positive sign.

"I'm loving your story about Kiko and the iguana."

So he doesn't hate iguanas.

"Thanks." I smile. Those are my favorite stories to write. The ones where there are seeds of truth mixed with lots of anything-is-possible.

"What do you think of *The Express*?" he asks as he scratches his beard, which is sort of black and sort of gray.

"I like it. The Dear Student column's the best part. So far my favorite is the one from Peanut Butter."

"I wanted to talk to you because I'd like you to be the new secret columnist for Dear Student."

Me?

I stare at him, my stomach spinning. "I thought you already picked someone."

Logan said it was happening this morning.

"I did," he says. "I picked you."

I shake my head. "No, I mean someone else. Someone who's not me."

"Why would you think that?"

"Everyone said you made your decision earlier today and probably picked an eighth grader."

"Well, everyone's wrong. I rotate the grade I choose from each year. It's important to get different perspectives. And this year, I wanted to pick a sixth grader."

"Oh."

"And that sixth grader is you," he says.

A smile slips out as I inhale my disbelief. But before I go to my happy place, I stare at his face, making sure his next words aren't "Just kidding."

But they aren't.

Then my insides light up like fireworks at the beach on the fourth of July.

"I think you've got the two things you need to give great advice," he says, taking another handful of chips.

"What's that?" I ask.

"Heart and honesty."

I smile. And my body fills with the kind of happiness that melts the hurt from a forgetful friend.

"Only thing you need to know is, if you take the job, it's a secret. No one at school can know it's you."

I nod.

"So, are you interested?" he asks.

20

Where Worries Sprout Like Dandelions

My heart feels like it used to when Dad and I made whoopie pies. I text him before I even leave school. I want him to know I did it! I found my one thing. Then I sprint home and fly into the kitchen.

"Hi," Mom says, taking off her reading glasses. "By the size of the smile spread across your face, looks like you had a great day."

"Yes!" I shout and spin around. "You're never going to believe what happened!"

I'm about to tell her that I'm Dear Student. That I seized the day. That I did it! Until Pickle walks into the room holding *Lady Pancake & Sir French Toast*. I look at my mom and sister and swallow my news. I can't share now. When I said yes to Mr. Baker, he reminded me of one big, important thing: Being the voice of Dear Student is a secret. No one at school can know it's me. Translation: I can't tell my little sister. The last secret I told her was about my crush on Jason Jameson, a boy who lived across the street when I was in fourth grade. Within twenty-four hours she'd shared with the check-out person at Rigley's Market, Mr. Higgins, our mail carrier, and everyone she saw on our block, including Jason Jameson.

"Yep, good day." Which is true if I exclude the part where my new friend forgot about my birthday. I hug my mom. She's wearing the soft green sweater Dad gave her for her birthday two years ago. I close my eyes and tuck in for an extra-long beat. I want to remember how happy she was that day. How happy we all were. But I can't. The memory's lost behind postcards and things that are temporary. Then I grab a yogurt, run to my room, and close the door.

I check my phone. No text from Dad yet.

"Spud, guess what?" I give him a celebratory slice of carrot. "I'm the new Dear Student!"

I text Prisha: *I got it! The Dear Student thing! I can't believe he picked me!* ♥♥♥♥

She texts back a GIF of a dancing guinea pig. And

Congrats! And then shares she got the lead in *Hairspray.*

You'll be amazing. I insert my happy Bitmoji—the one Logan helped me create. It's a girl with a brown braid, wearing an orange T-shirt with a picture of a dog on it. That was the only animal tee we could find.

My computer pings with a message from Mr. Baker.

I'm so glad you said yes. Here's an email that came into Dear Student after you left. Take a look.

I hold my breath and open the attachment.

> Dear Student,
>
> I'm terrible in math. I just don't get it. All the numbers blur into one big mound of I-have-no-idea-what-I'm-doing. I get help on one problem, then I get stuck all over again on the next one. Feeling like an idiot. What should I do?
>
> Sincerely,
>
> I-have-no-idea-what-I'm-doing

I reread the email. Okay. I love math. I can do this. I start to type.

My phone rings.

"So who do you think it is?" Logan blurts out.

I pause for a long minute.

"Wait. You're not still mad, are you?" She continues before I can answer. "I mean, I did say I'm sorry and we're going to celebrate your birthday at the dance. So I can't see why you'd be angry anymore."

I don't tell her that I was never really mad. Just sad. That being forgotten is the thing I'm most afraid of. I know this is a *me* thing. That it shouldn't be a big thing. She's right. She still wants to celebrate together. So I just say, "I'm not angry."

"Good. Now, who do you think it is?" she asks again.

"Who do I think what is?" I say, smelling the cinnamon spice aroma sticks Mom put in the room I share with Pickle so it smells less guinea pig and more sticky buns.

"Dear Student? I mean, I don't care that it's not me." She stops talking. "Well, maybe I care a little bit. But I'm way curious who Baker picked."

My stomach flips.

Do I say it's me?

"You still there?" Logan asks.

"Yep, still here."

"Maybe it's Jules and she was just asking if it was us to throw us off track?" Logan suggests.

In the well of my stomach where worries sprout like dandelions, I know I can't tell her that I'm Dear Student.

"I, um, guess. I mean, it could be Jules. But it's a secret anyway. So maybe we're not supposed to know."

Logan sighs. "Yeah. I guess. But I'd totally tell you."

I bite my lip and take another peek at the Dear Student email.

Baker said it had to be a secret. I'm not *allowed* to tell. That's the job.

I swallow the truth and say nothing.

She'll never find out it's me.

21

More Flapping Chicken Than Graceful Gazelle

I hang up with Logan and sit at the desk that was Dad's. I run my hands along the etched wood, take a deep breath, and inhale Fearless Fred.

Okay. Let's do this.

I start typing my first secret response as Dear Student. Then my brain sputters. *What if I can't figure out how to answer like a normal person in middle school?*

I shake my head, trying to remove the doubt that's creeping in.

Come on. You've got this.

I type some more.

But what if I get it wrong?

I delete.

Type.

What if people hate the advice I give?

Read it over.

Delete. It needs to be right.

Type again.

I read it one more time.

Maybe it doesn't sound terrible or weird or wrong. I actually kind of like it. I smile. Maybe I *can* do this. I attach my answer to an email, hold my breath, and send my first response as Dear Student to Mr. Baker.

I did it!

Then my phone pings with a text from Dad: *Way to go!*

I stare at the words, hoping he's proud of me. The kind of proud that means he's coming home for our birthdays and maybe forever. I grab my orange striped comforter from the floor and toss it over my legs.

Another email from Mr. Baker. *Loved your advice to I-have-no-idea-what-I'm-doing! Attached are a few more.*

He liked my advice! I've got this! I open the next letter.

Dear Student,

What do you think: Country or electronic dance music at the dance?

Signed,
Cowboy Hat

This one's harder. I've never been to a school dance and my dance moves are more flapping chicken than graceful gazelle. What do I do now? I look around my room. Nothing here to help. But YouTube is filled with kids posting playlists and jams from their middle school dances. I slide in my earbuds, listen, and watch. Then write.

Dear Cowboy Hat,

I guess I know what gets your boots out on the dance floor. Like you, I love some good C&W with an orange flannel. But we're going to need to play some EDM to get everyone dancing!

Sincerely,
Student

I hit Send and pull up the next one.

Dear Student,

My best friend doesn't really seem like my best friend anymore. We didn't have a fight. Nothing happened. That's the weird part. But she's always busy when I ask her to do anything. And she doesn't talk to me much at school anymore. She doesn't full-on ignore me, but she only smiles or waves when she's alone. Feel like if I say anything, she'll totally bail.

What should I do?

Signed,
Feeling Ditched

I stare at the words and think about Prisha and how grateful I am that distance hasn't changed us.

Dear Feeling Ditched,

I'm no friend guru, but I'd talk to her. One of two things will happen: Either she'll realize she's being a jerk, will apologize, and you'll have your BFF back. Or she won't apologize. Because right now she is a jerk. And you're better off without her.

Signed,

Student

I cross my fingers and hope with all the power in Pickle's cape that the BFF apologizes. I open the last email.

Dear Student,

I just found out there's a cosmetics company that's moving into town that uses animals to test their new products. Animals! I'm so angry and super worried. I have a pet, and my best friend has a pet like the one they test on! I tried writing to the company, but they didn't respond. Now we need to do something.

Can you help?

Sincerely,

Super Worried

The air seeps out of my room.

I stare at the photo on the desk of me and Pickle with Spud in the yard. He looks supercute, with a dandelion on his head.

I reread the letter. My brain fogs.

I walk over to Spud and rub the soft fur between his ears. "Who could ever do something like that to you?"

22

Spuds of the World

I wake up thinking about Super Worried and Dear Student. My response is swimming in my brain. Somewhere. I just need to figure out what to say to protect the Spuds of the world.

I grab a banana on my way out of the house, and when I walk into English, I spy Logan. I bet she'd know what to tell Super Worried. I wish I could ask her. But I already know I can't.

She's wearing a tie-dye T-shirt. I look down at my mud-brown one with a giant frog on the front and a drip of sad slides in. They don't match. Not that we had a matching plan for today, but I liked being connected in that small way. It kind of felt like our own orange ribbon.

She smiles and I wave. Behind my back I cross my fingers and hope she doesn't ask me again about Dear Student. I know I'm doing the right thing, but every time I have to not-answer, it makes me queasy from my high-tops to my head. Thankfully, Mr. Baker dives right into a long discussion about themes in *The Vanderbeekers of 141st Street.*

When Baker's class ends, I don't go to the stadium-size cafeteria to talk about the clothes I don't own that I should wear to the dance that I don't want to go to. Instead, I head straight to the science lab to meet Cooper. I invited Logan, but she was a solid no. Followed by "I hate science."

When I walk in, Ms. Murphy waves and I notice her earrings that look like beakers. I wave back. Cooper isn't here yet, so I pull up Super Worried's email. I think about Spud, and Superman, Sugar, Wilbur, and all the animals at Hillview Vet, and don't understand how anyone could hurt them on purpose.

Dear Super Worried,

Hooray for your willingness to act! Lots of people feel compassion for animals but aren't able to do something about it.

Like me.

What about making flyers to create awareness?

What else? Anyone can make flyers.

What would Fearless Fred do?

Then I know.

> What about a march? An organized protest to stop the company and save the animals.
>
> Signed,
> Student

That's it! I read it over and happiness floods my insides. A march is the way to protect all the Spuds of the world. I hit Send.

Cooper joins me at the table. I close my laptop and take out my bagel and cream cheese.

"So, when do you want to make that video of Superman?" he says, sitting across from me.

"How about Friday after school? We can meet at the picnic table in front of Hillview Vet."

"Cool. I think this will totally work." He takes his just-peanut-butter sandwich out of his brown paper bag. "I had a friend in D.C. who lost his grandfather's watch and found it when someone posted about it online."

I nod and spread more cream cheese on my bagel.

Then he says, "Now that we have a plan to find Superman's owner, any chance you can help me find a job?"

I open a bag of gummies and offer him some. "What kind of job?"

"Anything." He takes red, orange, and green gummy frogs.

"There's a family down our street with three little kids. They're always looking for help."

"The last time I babysat, I started a small fire in the family's toaster oven."

"Okay. Not babysitting."

"I've applied all over, but no one will hire me. They won't even let me bag groceries at Rigley's Market. Some dumb rule about needing to be fourteen." He downs the rest of his milk, the only other thing in his lunch bag, and continues talking. "My mom said if I want to keep Mr. Magoo, I need to take care of him. And to take care of him, I need money. And if I need money, I need a job."

The bright purple nail polish Logan convinced me looks great stares up at me. I tuck my hands in my lap.

"Any ideas?" he asks, running his fingers through his spiky buzz cut.

I finish my bagel and hope there aren't any seeds stuck in my teeth as I roll the tinfoil into a ball. "What about selling something? Like lemonade?"

"That could work." He stands up and paces around Mr. Bean, the skeleton. "But I saw two lemonade stands the other day. Neither was busy." He turns toward me. "What about cookies?"

"Maybe." My mind spins. I'm a good baker. Mostly. Except for cookies. In third grade, I burnt the hamantaschen I was making for the Purim party at Grandma Bea's temple. I had to buy some at the bakery on the way to the party. Dressed as Queen Esther.

"What if we sold whoopie pies?" I say, staring at Mr. Bean. "I mean, not we, but you, as in only you. But I, um, just know how to make really good ones. I used to make them with my dad."

He stops pacing and looks at me.

"I could show you. Or just send you the recipe."

I feel the hives threatening to flood my neck.

Stop talking.

He shoves the rest of his sandwich in his mouth, swallows, and says, "That's perfect! We can do it together."

The bell rings.

My hives retreat.

23

Clumsy Robot

I'm fully committed to not going to the dance tonight, but Logan won't let me ditch.

"I promise it'll be great," she says as we head to our lockers at the end of school.

"I can't dance," I confess, thinking it's better to tell her now before she witnesses my awkwardness on full display tonight. "Think clumsy robot. Then put my face on it. That's me dancing."

She laughs. "I'm sure it's not that bad. You can just do what I do."

Like that would work.

"Look, I'll even come over now. We can practice and I can help you pick out what to wear."

The thought of Logan rummaging through my closet of animal T-shirts to find a worthy middle school dance outfit feels like an episode of *Survivor* meets *Naked and Afraid*. But it doesn't matter anyway, because I have to meet Cooper.

"Huge thanks. But I can't."

Her face scrunches up. "Why?"

"I'm, um, doing this thing with, um, Cooper at Hillview Vet to find Superman's owner." I don't know why it feels awkward telling her. I'm not doing anything wrong. But somehow it still feels like I am.

"Oh," she pauses. "Anyway, you *have* to come to the dance after that because we're celebrating your birthday." She grabs my hand. "I know I messed up before. But I really want to do this together."

Her voice sounds like she means it and my heart twists. "Okay. I promise I'll be at the dance," I say. Grateful to have a friend who lives in my time zone who wants to do stuff with me. Even if it's stuff I don't want to do.

Then she leans in close and whispers, "Besides, I found out this thing and need your help."

I pop a handful of green gummy frogs into my mouth, hoping what she found out isn't the identity of the secret voice of Dear Student.

"This thing I'm going to tell you is bad, Autumn. Really bad."

"Just say it. You're scaring me." I hate the gap between not knowing and knowing. It feels like I'm plummeting down a dark, bottomless well.

"Remember the company Beautiful You that we were talking about the other day when we were with my mom in the car? The one with all the jobs?"

I nod, picking the purple polish off my pinkie nail.

"That company tests their products on animals." I stop picking the nail polish and swallow hard. *Is this the same company that Super Worried was talking about?*

Logan's voice is all serious business. "They say they do it for safety reasons. You know, so when people wear their lipstick, mascara, and eye shadow, they won't get sick or break out in some gross rash."

"I get that no one wants to be covered in a bumpy rash, but testing on innocent animals is just wrong." I pause. "Wait. What kind of animals do they use?" My heart races as the words escape my mouth. I've been thinking about this ever since I got that email from Super Worried.

"Mice, rats, rabbits, dogs, and, um," Logan pauses, "guinea pigs."

Fear hammers my insides.

"I've already tried writing to the company, but they never responded," Logan says.

I bite my lip.

"I don't know what else to do," she says.

A prickly feeling climbs across my chest.

In that moment, I realize Logan *is* Super Worried.

She wrote that email to Dear Student. The one *I* responded to.

Now I cross my fingers and hope that she likes the advice I gave.

And never finds out that I'm the one who gave it to her.

Pet Monkey Named Potato

My brain's spinning about Dear Student and Super Worried. But I can't think about any of that right now. I'm meeting Cooper and I'm late.

I race over to Banana Splitz for two orders of the best mint chip ice cream with hot fudge, and when I walk back with the ice cream, Cooper's already sitting at the red picnic table in front of Hillview Vet. I love this table. It reminds me of picnics with Grandma Bea when I was a little girl. That's who I got my love of animals and strawberry banana cream pie from. There's a photograph on the kitchen counter of Grandma Bea with her pet monkey, Potato, whose name was really Pete. But no one called him Pete after he dug up all the potatoes in Grandpa Jack's garden.

I give Cooper his sundae and slide in across from him.

We talk about his favorite comic book shop in D.C., his best friend, Nico, and Mr. Magoo. While I'm telling him about the pet monkey named Potato, Logan walks over. "Hi," she says, plucking the cherry from the top of my sundae and eating it.

Oh. Okay. I didn't really want that anyway.

"I'm Logan," she says to Cooper, full of smiles and aren't-you-happy-to-meet-me.

He smiles. "Cooper."

Logan takes a spoonful of my ice cream. "This is so good." She wipes her mouth with my napkin. "Why didn't you tell me you were down for ice cream? I'd have totally met you guys."

I swallow hard, not knowing how to answer this.

"It's all good," Logan says, waving her hands in the air. "I had to drop off something for Snow White and figured I'd run into you anyway." She moves in next to me. "Plus, I wanted to see if you changed your mind about me helping you get ready for the dance."

My face gets hot. "Thanks. You're the best," I say, not wanting to hurt her feelings. "But honest, I'm good."

She shrugs. "You going to the dance?" she asks Cooper.

I stare at him, hoping it's a yes.

"Dances aren't really my thing."

He says it so easily, like he doesn't care if anyone thinks it's weird.

Logan nods. "Wait, I know you. You're the science lab kid." He looks at her confused. "The one Autumn has lunch with."

I bite my lip. *Why did she say that?* I don't want Cooper thinking I'm talking about him to my friend.

She takes another bite of my ice cream and stands up. "That explains it."

"Explains what?" he says.

"Why you aren't going to the dance."

"Not really," he says. "I can like science and dances. I just don't."

"Whatever," she says. Then she turns her attention back to me. "See you tonight. I can't wait."

"Me too," I say, hoping that sounds more excited than I feel. Then I ask her if she wants to make the video with us. I don't know why I didn't ask her earlier. But she says no. And as she walks away, I pray that navigating two friends doesn't always feel like a colony of ants marching across my body.

Cooper and I head inside Hillview Vet to visit Superman.

"Nice ladybug tattoo," he says, dimple showing.

My face turns the color of the cherry Logan ate as I slide my sleeve down to hide the tattoo. This morning, Pickle asked if she could put a stick-on ladybug on my right arm. Then she put one on hers so we'd be twins.

We find our iguana friend and give him some collard greens. Then we make a video with him, asking if anyone's missing this guy. It takes a few tries because I can't stop laughing. Superman won't let Cooper pick him up. Finally, I step in with the gloves Mom gave me and scoop up Superman. Once we finish the video, Cooper posts it online with Hillview Vet as the contact.

"Glad we did this. Totally hope his owner sees it," Cooper says, getting up. "Have fun at the dance."

I wave goodbye to my friend.

Then race back upstairs to get ready for a dance I don't want to go to.

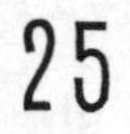

Almost True

An hour later I'm standing in the gym with my nerves hiding under my new penguin T-shirt. I don't want to talk about Dear Student or Beautiful You or the fact that I'm keeping all this from my new BFF. Before I left the house, I wove my orange ribbon into my braid. I wanted a little piece of Prisha with me.

"Oh, I love this song," Logan says, grabbing my hand. "Come on." She pulls me out to a group of kids on the dance floor.

My nerves snap. I look around at all the smiling people who like this and realize I'll never be one of those people.

"I'm going to get some water," I say to Logan.

"Just follow my lead," she whispers, pushing back her sparkly headband.

"It's not that," I say, which is almost true because I am superthirsty.

I leave the dance floor, look back, and see the circle of friends closing in around Logan. I take a drink of water, find a bleacher to sit on, and pull out my phone.

I'm trying to beat my high score in Bubble Crush when an email from Mr. Baker comes in with more Dear Student letters. I close my game and open the email, hoping it's not about companies that try to hurt animals.

> Dear Student,
>
> Apple pie vs. pumpkin pie.
>
> Where do you fall?
>
> Signed,
>
> Slice

I exhale, thankful for pie. Then I think of the crickets at Logan's house and am pretty sure they won't be in the running for best pie.

Dear Slice,

Strawberry banana cream would be my write-in favorite. But if I had to choose between apple and pumpkin, I'd be #teamapple.

Sincerely,

Student

I read it over and decide it sounds like something someone in middle school might say.

The next song comes on and I look up expecting to see Logan running over to pull me back onto the dance floor. But she isn't. She's dancing in a new circle with girls I don't know.

A blend of disappointment and relief slides in. I don't want to dance. But I kind of want her to want me to dance. Which is confusing.

So I move on to the next Dear Student email.

Dear Student,

Help! I'm crushing on someone, but worried they're crushing on someone else. What do I do?

Sincerely,

Crushed

My brain freezes because my biggest crush was in fourth grade on Jason Jameson. It takes me a while to figure out what to say and how to say it in a way that sounds like I know what I'm talking about. I listen to the music and start writing.

Dear Crushed,

We can't help who we crush on, but we can help what we do about it. If your crush isn't crushing back, move on.

Sincerely,
Student

I read it back. Sounds upbeat and empowered. That's what *Girl Power* magazine said about helping a friend through a breakup. I know this isn't technically a breakup, but I figure it's close enough.

I send my responses to Mr. Baker and my phone pings a text from Cooper.

At Hillview Vet. Something's wrong with Mr. Magoo

My heart races.

What happened?

He texts right back. *Not sure. After I left you, I went home. He got into my mom's stuff, so I took him outside. Didn't notice anything weird. But then his body started shaking and his eyes did this thing where they looked like they were rolling around. Wasn't sure where else to go*

The music feels like it's in the way of my brain. I step outside the gym. The hall is bright, but quiet.

I text Cooper. *On my way*

That wasn't what I was planning to text. But it shot out before I could take it back.

I open the door to the gym and walk onto the dance floor.

"Yay! You're here," Logan says. "Dance with me."

"I, um, actually need to leave."

Logan stops. "Why?"

"Cooper's dog is sick."

"So?" Logan says, taking off the speckled glasses that match her T-shirt.

"He's at Hillview Vet and I thought I should go there. You know. He's worried."

"But you were with him all afternoon," she says.

I nod, unsure what that has to do with this.

"And we didn't get to celebrate your birthday yet. I was waiting. You know, until later." She smiles, putting her glasses back on.

I don't say anything because there's a tiny part of me that wonders if that's really true. She hasn't mentioned it once since I got here.

"Besides, what are you even going to do there? You're not a vet."

"He's alone. I thought I'd wait with him."

"Whatever," she says as she turns back to the group of kids dancing and singing along with the music.

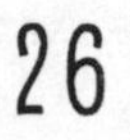

26

Bad Endings

I text Mom that I'm heading to Hillview Vet. That's the deal with the new phone. I get some independence, but I need to tell her about it. Which I think isn't really what it means to be independent.

I walk through the big yellow door and see Cooper talking to my mom by the front desk. They don't see me.

"You did the right thing bringing him here," Mom says. "Is your mother meeting you?"

He shakes his head. "Not sure. I left her a message."

"Okay. Don't worry. We'll take good care of Mr. Magoo."

"Can I, um, talk to you?" he asks my mom, looking around. "In private."

My mom nods and the two of them disappear down the hall.

Bear runs over to me and leans in for some love and an ear rub. Just like he used to whenever Dad showed up. I wonder if he misses Dad's bristly beard and hair gel that smells like grapefruit. If he wishes every night that Dad will come back. I hand Bear a chicken-flavored treat and whisper in his ear, "Fingers and paws crossed he'll be home soon." I texted Dad again last night, reminding him about our birthday party and that Pickle really misses him. No word yet.

I hug Bear and visit Sugar the tarantula, who's creeping across her cage. Then I find a quiet corner next to Superman and flop onto the beanbag chair Dad and I bought together before he left. Sitting here makes me feel closer to him. When he first left, I could still smell the grapefruit when I went into the bathroom that he and Mom shared. Made me feel like he wasn't really gone. Then we moved and the smell disappeared.

While I wait, I find the picture of Spud I took yesterday and make a list on my phone of his most important features just in case he ever gets lost, like Superman did.

One-year-old guinea pig named Spud:

1. Loves carrots
2. Is kind of fat (probably from too many carrots)
3. Orange and white
4. Pink nose
5. Black button eyes
6. Kind of sharp toenails (because I hate cutting them)
7. Looks like a giant baked potato

"I just saw your text." It's Cooper. "Thanks for coming."

"How's Mr. Magoo?" I ask.

"Not good."

"What happened?"

"Not sure. He got into my mom's purse. She got mad, so I took him outside. Didn't notice him eating anything strange, but when we went back inside, he started shaking and not answering when I called his name." His voice cracks. "Then his eyes did this weird thing."

I grab two boxes of Junior Mints from the vending machine and we sit with Superman while we wait for answers about Mr. Magoo.

Cooper pours some mints into his hand. "I was thinking maybe we could do the whoopie pie thing soon. Taking care of Mr. Magoo has just gotten really expensive."

I bite my lip. "Sure." We make a plan and I hope my whoopie pies are as good as Dad's. Then my phone buzzes. *Miss you,* Logan texts with hearts under a pic of her, Jules, Evie, and Maya on the dance floor. I'm about to text back a pic of Superman when Mom slides a chair over and hands Cooper and me each a water bottle. "Mr. Magoo needs to stay here for a couple of days," she tells Cooper in her serious voice.

"What happened to him?" Cooper asks.

"I think he ingested some kind of poison and we need to see if he responds to a lipid treatment."

My mind spins back to Beautiful You. What if they threw out stuff that was poisonous and Mr. Magoo accidentally ate it?

"But he's going to be okay. Right?" Cooper asks, his eyes brimming with bad endings.

I stare at my mother. *Please-don't-say-the-really-terrible-thing.*

She pauses and says, "I don't have the answer to that question yet."

I hate this part.

"But, um —" Cooper's voice cracks.

Mom interrupts, "Mr. Magoo can stay as long as he needs to."

I search online. Apparently, lipids are fat that can pull certain poisons out of the system. But since Mom's not sure what poison Mr. Magoo got into, she can't know for sure if the treatment will work.

Cooper paces and I pull out my phone again. My words need an escape hatch.

> Kiko worries when she can't turn her invisibility power back on. She tries three more times, but it's not working. She knows what happened. Max must have told her secret. That's the only way to deactivate the power. Kiko looks in the mirror. She doesn't want to be seen. She feels bare and exposed, like she's glowing in the dark. She curls into a ball next to Apollo, not sure she's ready for all the light.

I put my phone away and find Malcolm on the computer at the front desk. He tells me there are no updates on whether or not the lipid treatment's working yet.

I try to think of something helpful to say to Cooper, but I can't come up with anything that will make him stop pacing. Then he says, "I'm sorry," like we've been talking.

"For what?" I ask.

"The thing I said the other day on the beach." He stops pacing. "Mr. Magoo isn't the only good thing about moving here."

I pray he can't see the red I feel spreading across my cheeks.

My phone buzzes. It's Logan. Wishing me a happy birthday. In all the worries over Mr. Magoo, I hadn't realized it was already past midnight.

Today slipped in unnoticed.

Another buzz. I'm about to turn my phone off when I realize it's a text from Prisha. A happy birthday video of a dancing guinea pig and a cake with candles. I laugh.

"What's so funny?" Cooper wants to know.

My heart races. I show him the message from Prisha, hoping it doesn't seem babyish or weird.

He smiles. "Happy birthday."

I fidget in my seat. "Thanks."

Mom walks over. "Mr. Magoo's responding well to the treatment."

I hear Cooper release a scared breath.

"Your dog will stay here, but it's time I brought you home. I gave your mom a call and told her I'd give you a ride."

We pile into the truck, and Mom follows Cooper's directions to his apartment building. It's a four-story redbrick building with a sign out front that says YOU ARE HOME. Cooper thanks my mom, hops out of the car, and disappears inside.

Mom turns to me. "Happy birthday, Autumn."

"Thanks, Mom."

The ride home is quiet. When we get there, I wave to Malcolm, who's babysitting Pickle. This is usually my job, but when I'm gone, Malcolm fills in. Pickle says he's her favorite because he lets her stay up late and eat as many pickles as she wants.

I hug Spud, thankful he didn't get into any mystery poison. Then I fall asleep.

Pickle wakes me way too early. When I open my eyes, she's in full birthday attire. Lime-green cape, crown, and pink sneakers. "Happy birthday to us. Happy birthday to us. Happy birthday dear Autumn and Pickle, happy birthday to us!" she sings.

She hands me a present wrapped in her pale-yellow blanket.

"I couldn't find wrapping paper," she says.

"It's perfect." I sit up, tuck my stuffed platypus, Pepper, next to me, and unwrap my gift.

Sitting in the middle of my little sister's baby blanket is a bright orange cape.

"You're Super Sister!" Pickle says. "My superhero."

27

I Don't Care

"Happy birthday to us!" Pickle says, handing me my Super Sister cape. Then she puts a cardboard crown with a gold star on top of my head. She got two matching ones when we went to Bellow's Arcade. I gave her all the tickets I won playing Skee-Ball and she exchanged them at the prize counter for two crowns.

I put on my crown. "I know. I promise I won't be late." I look at my clock, thinking it's almost time for Dad to surprise us. I bet he's going to do it at the party. My whole body smiles. I figured it out last night while I was waiting with Cooper. I realized the reason Dad hasn't said a word about our birthdays must be because he's coming home to surprise us.

I get ready and still have time before I need to meet Mom and Pickle. I open my computer and there's a new email from Mr. Baker with more Dear Student letters attached.

> Dear Student,
>
> My sister is in the army and is being deployed next month. I'm going to miss her. I want to give her something to remember me by. Any ideas?
>
> Sincerely,
> Remember Me

I run my fingers along my *hamsa* and remember how Grandma Bea always smelled like coffee, wore her hair in a tight bun, and sang loudly whenever we went to temple together. Then I think about Dad and his postcards and the way he writes my name.

Dear Remember Me,

How about a handwritten letter from you that she can tuck in her pack? That way, she gets to hold on to your words and your handwriting.

Sincerely,
Student

I move on to the next email.

Dear Student,

I have two friends who each want something different and only one of their wants can happen. How do I choose between friends?

Sincerely,
Torn

I bite my lip. I get how hard it is to have friends who want different things. I think about Cooper and Logan and am thankful that science and dances are the only things they disagree on.

I hold my breath and send my responses to Mr. Baker. Then I head into the kitchen. Mom smiles at me and the crown that I forgot was still on my head. She kisses my cheek and hands me a plate with a large slice of strawberry banana cream pie on it. "A gift from Malcolm," Mom says. "Happy birthday."

I look at her, wondering if she's going to slip and say something about the surprise. But she doesn't. She probably doesn't want to ruin it. She just smiles and puts a small orange box on the table. Inside is a ring that looks like rope. She holds out her hand and is wearing the same ring on her pinkie. "When life zigs and zags, I want you to know that we'll get through it together. I'll always be here for you. Our hearts are interwoven."

"Thanks, Mom." I slip the ring on my pinkie. "I love it."

My phone rings. It's Dad, full of birthday wishes and happiness.

This. Is. It.

I stand up and look around. "Where are you?" I bet he's hiding downstairs at Hillview Vet, or maybe he's behind the broken dryer, or in Mom's room, waiting for the right moment to step out and surprise me.

"What do you mean?" he says.

My breath catches in the back of my throat.

"I'm in Ecuador."

Disappointment floods my heart.

He's not hiding.

"I, um, thought you were coming," I say in a cracked voice.

"Where?" he asks.

"Home." The word sounds weird on my tongue.

"I will." He coughs. "Eventually."

His words floats untethered in the air.

"I know this isn't a big birthday. It's not like my bat mitzvah year or even when I turned double digits, but still. I thought you'd want to be here."

"Of course I want to be with you. I just couldn't make it work right now." He goes on to tell me how much he loves and misses me. But I've already stopped believing him. I hand the phone to Pickle who dances while our dad sings "Happy Birthday." I go to our room and lie on my bed with Spud.

Mom comes in. "You okay?"

I shake my head.

She hugs me as tears roll down my cheeks.

"I thought he was coming," I say.

"I'm sorry."

"He's the one who should be apologizing. He left. You stayed." I sit up and let out a big breath of sadness. "I just don't get why we aren't enough."

"You're always enough," she says, taking my hand in hers. "And he loves you." She pauses. "I'm not saying that makes it hurt less. I'm just saying he does."

"I'm not sure that's enough anymore." I pause. "It shouldn't be enough for you either. I'm not the only one he left behind."

"I know." Her voice is laced with a hurt I know she's hiding. Last week I saw a bunch of texts between her and Dad. She told him she was sad and mad and missed him. That we missed him. That it was time for him to come home.

"Sometimes we do things for the people we love."

"But that has to go both ways," I say.

She nods. Then she puts her hands on my chin so I need to look her in the eyes. "I agree with you, Autumn, it does go both ways. And I'm not happy with your dad right now either. But today isn't about him. It's about you and your sister." She smiles at me, and I see the lines around her eyes. "And I want to celebrate my amazing daughters."

I wipe my cheeks, hug my mom, and tell her I'll be down soon. I take out my checked notebook with the frayed edges and write the words I couldn't say to my dad. I look up at the water-stained ceiling in my temporary room and make my birthday wish.

I want my dad to come home.

But more than that, I want my dad to want to come home.

28

Pin the Tail on the Iguana

Just before noon, Mom, Pickle, and I head downstairs to Hillview Vet for the party. Pickle's friends Kamal and Ryan—the boy down the street who doesn't talk a lot—and Malcolm and Bear join us for our birthday celebration with Wilbur and Flame and Spud. I hand out chocolate cupcakes with extra sprinkles and strawberry banana cream pie to all our two-legged guests. Turns out Malcolm made two pies. One for breakfast and one for the party.

Pickle wants me to show everyone my new birthday present. I grab my bright orange cape, drape it across my shoulders, twirl, and laugh. I stop worrying about being forgotten. I stop worrying about doing and saying the right thing. I stop worrying about everything.

Malcolm and Mom cheer loudly and Pickle hops up and down, clapping. I hand her a package wrapped in striped paper. Her bright eyes sparkle as she tears the paper off to find a jar. An empty jar.

"I love it!" She tilts her head to the side. "What is it?"

I laugh. "A superpower jar. Any time you feel scared or worried, you put those feelings on a piece of paper and slip them into the jar."

Her eyes widen. "Then what?"

"The jar fills with all the superpower you'll need to find Fearless Fred so you won't be scared or worried."

"Really?"

I nod and cross my fingers behind my back, hoping my first act as Super Sister works.

Pickle hugs me tight with her chocolate cupcake hands. "I love my jar!"

My phone pings. Text from Logan: *Sorry not there. Hope party's a blast*

I mute my phone and shove it back in my pocket. I go over to Bear, who's stretched across the tile floor, and rub between his ears. "Thanks for coming." He nuzzles my hand. Not confusing at all.

Pickle and her friends play Pin the Tail on the Iguana.

I slip in to see Mr. Magoo and find my mom checking on him, too. "He looks good," she says.

"Any idea what made him so sick?" I ask.

She shakes her head. "I wish I did. Right now, I'm just grateful the lipid treatment is working."

I kiss Mr. Magoo's cold nose. "What did Cooper want to talk to you about in private?"

"You know I can't share that information, Autumn. That's between me and my patient."

"Well, technically, Mr. Magoo's your patient."

She laughs. "You have a point, but either way, if Cooper wanted to share it, he wouldn't have asked to speak to me alone."

I nod and pet Mr. Magoo's belly until Pickle shows up holding a piece of paper with a picture of a smiley face with a beard and long hair in a ponytail.

"It's Dad," she says. "I'm going to put it in my jar. Then I won't worry that he's going to forget me."

I wrap my little sister in my arms. "He won't forgot you, Pickle." I hear the words I'm saying and hope the magic in the Super Jar lets us both believe them. Because after the phone call with him this morning, I worry he's so happy seizing the day in Ecuador, he's forgotten how much he misses us.

When she lets go of me, she says, "Oh. Your friend is here."

"What friend?"

She shrugs and skips away.

I wind down the hall to the main entrance.

Standing there is Logan. "Happy birthday!" she says.

"I thought you were at the social justice meeting thing," I say, freaking out on the inside. I never told her this wasn't a party.

"You're kind of terrible with your new phone," she says, sliding her sparkly blue headband back.

I never told her there'd be no other kids our age here.

"I texted you."

I glance at my phone. Four missed texts from Logan.

Leaving meeting early to come to party 🎉 🍰

K? 🙍‍♀️

You still there? 😳

On my way 🚘

She looks around. "Where is everyone?"

I take in what she sees. Her friend in a crown and

bright orange cape. Her friend's mom waving too enthusiastically from across the room. A few little kids and lots of weird animals scattered through the hall.

"Am I too late?" she asks.

I slide off my crown and fumble to untie my cape as dread wraps itself around me.

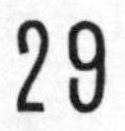

29

The Whole Truth

"You're not too late," I say, my stomach dropping to the ugly brown floor.

"But no one's here." Logan looks around. "I mean, like, no one our age."

I think I might throw up.

"Where is everyone?" she asks.

"This *is* everyone," I say, trying to swallow the humiliation that comes when your new friend sees your embarrassing truth.

Long pause filled with chunks of uncomfortable drifts between us.

Pickle rushes over with a tray. "Want a chocolate

cupcake with extra sprinkles or Autumn's favorite, strawberry banana cream pie?"

"Thanks," Logan says, taking a cupcake.

"Pickle, this is my, um, friend Logan."

Pickle smiles, chocolate icing stuck to her front teeth. "Did you know my sister and I have the exact same birthday and every year we have a party together?"

"I didn't know that." Logan looks at me. "But it's really cool."

It is?

"Wish I shared a birthday with someone."

"It's the best!" Pickle says, running off to join her friends.

Logan turns to me. "Why didn't you tell me?"

"Because you weren't coming."

"Even before I wasn't coming, you didn't tell me."

"I wasn't sure you'd come if I told you."

There it is, the whole truth.

"Wow! That stings," Logan says.

I stare at my friend. Her face looks sad, but her voice sounds kind of mad. Which confuses me.

"You talked like I was having this big thing, even when I said it was going to be small," I say. "So I was kind of embarrassed."

"I thought that was why you didn't want me to say anything to our friends the other day."

"I didn't want you to say anything because I wasn't sure everyone—or *anyone*—would get this." I point to the Pin the Tail on the Iguana, the cupcakes, the five-year-olds, the animals. "I thought maybe kids like you do, um, different parties."

"What do you mean, kids like me?" she asks, her blue eyes squinty and serious behind her black-rimmed glasses.

"You know, the ones who are friends with everyone." The ones who always know what to say. What to do. Never feel awkward. Or weird. Or out of place.

She shakes her head. "I'm not friends with everyone. I'm trying to figure it out. Just like you."

I stare at Logan. On the outside she's like her sparkly sneakers. But maybe on the inside she's more like me.

Logan takes a bite of the chocolate cupcake.

Or maybe it doesn't matter if she's like me. Maybe all that matters is that she likes chocolate cupcakes and birthdays.

And me.

"Anyway, these are seriously amazing," Logan says, taking another bite of her cupcake.

I smile. "Thanks."

We walk to the back to give Flame some dandelion greens and Wilbur a carrot. I rub Wilbur's snout. "You know, potbellied pigs only sweat through their noses."

Logan nods and I bite my lip, hoping that wasn't a weird thing to say. Then, "What happened at the social justice meeting? Did your mom get to see you do your thing?"

"Not exactly." Logan stops and looks at me. "It ended early. She didn't come."

"Why?"

"She had something important," she says. "A big case she's working on."

"Oh."

"My mom says it's work that's making a difference. So, I get it," Logan says.

But she's wearing her sad eyebrows. Which kind of looks the way I felt when Dad said he wasn't coming home. So I'm not sure I believe her.

I hug my friend. Tie my cape around her neck and slip my hand in hers.

30

Weirdo

Logan and I spend every afternoon together this week. We even video call Prisha on Thursday after school from Logan's room. I want my BFFs to meet. Even if they're totally different. Prisha is just like me except she likes to dance, and Logan is, well, nothing like me.

When I wake up Saturday morning, Mom's making waffles. That's how I know it's a beach day. Even before I open my eyes, the smell floods my room in the best possible way. I hop out of bed and follow the sweet scent to the kitchen.

Mom hands me a waffle straight from Dad's old waffle maker. I take a bite, which tastes as delicious as it smells.

Which isn't always true. When I was four, I tried my kiwi shampoo, which didn't taste anything like it smelled.

I'm not sure why waffles and beach go together, but Mom says they do. And always have. She says it has to do with her father, Grandpa Jack. Same thing. Waffles and beach. Then she points to the bag in the corner. "Ladder ball, boogie boards, and lunch packed and ready to go."

I know Mom's doing this to make us feel like we're still a happy family even though twenty-five percent of us isn't here.

Pickle spins in her rainbow bathing suit and flip-flops and hands me a handful of dandelions she found this morning. She tells me her Superpower Jar works. "Today, I read all the words on the page. I mean, Mom helped, but I did it!"

I give her a thumbs-up. "Way to go!"

"Also, the other day at school, the pet hamster got stuck in her tube," Pickle says, and laughs with her whole body.

When Mom sits at the kitchen table, she has her coffee mug in one hand and a new postcard in the other. On the front is a picture of lots of hats.

Hello from one of the most incredible places in the world. I love Ecuador! In honor of your birthdays, I visited a

Panama hat factory and got you each a white hat with a black band. Can't wait to give them to you.

How was the cupcake celebration this year? Sorry I couldn't make it. But I was thinking of my favorite girls.

Miss you both.

Your Loving Dad

"I love hats!" Pickle says.

"Don't hold your breath," I say to my little sister.

Her bottom lip quivers.

"Autumn, don't do that," Mom says.

"What? Be honest?" I turn to Pickle. "Dad's not coming home."

Pickle starts to cry.

"That's not true," Mom says, her face flushed.

"It feels true," I say as I leave to go to my room. I look back and see my mother hugging my little sister.

I'm done pretending we're still a family of four.

Because we're not.

My phone buzzes. It's Logan. "My parents are gone for the day. Please save me from Mrs. Yard—the sitter my mom insisted is coming over to check on me—and say we can hang out."

I think of Logan with Mrs. Yard, which is weirdly the same as being alone, and say, "We're going to King's Beach. I can ask if you can come."

"Yes, please!" she says.

Mom tells me it's fine for Logan to join us as long as I apologize to Pickle first. But while she's talking, I wonder if this is really a good idea. She's putting on a sun hat with a brim the size of a small flying saucer. Then I remember Logan's already seen Pin the Tail on the Iguana and me wearing my bright orange cape and think things couldn't get much more embarrassing.

Before we leave, I find Pickle and say I'm sorry. It's not her fault that Dad's gone.

An hour later, Mom's setting up a large pop-up tent to block the sun that isn't somehow already shielded by her ginormous hat. Logan's two-piece bathing suit is pink and blue and supercute. I look down at my navy one-piece and tug on the bottom. Mom says it's great that it still fits even though I got it two years ago.

I'm not sure *great* is the word I'd use. I keep my turtle T-shirt on.

Logan leans over. "Let's go for a walk on the beach."

My mom's lathering up with sunblock like she's preparing for Armageddon. "Logan and I are heading down to the jetties," I say like it's normal. Like it's not the first time I'd be doing this without a parent. Then I hold my breath and look at my mom.

Please don't say anything embarrassing.

"Okay. Just don't be long."

Exhale.

Logan gets up and slips on her sunglasses.

I put on my SAVE THE WHALES cap.

"Can I come? I want to look for snails," Pickle says.

"Maybe you and Mom can look for snails here," I say.

But Pickle is already holding Logan's hand.

"It's cool," Logan says.

The three of us walk along the edge of the waves, and after a while, Pickle gives me her bucket and tells me that she needs to pee in the ocean. We spend the next hour collecting hermit crabs and snails and building a sandcastle with a moat. When Pickle's hungry, we bring her back to Mom and turkey sandwiches, and Logan and I go for a swim. Alone.

"My mom said she's free tomorrow and we could do something the three of us. Not sure what it will be, but want to come?" Logan asks.

I promised Cooper we'd do the whoopie pies tomorrow. But maybe Logan can do it with us. "I can't come over, but—"

"Why?"

"I told Cooper I'd do this thing with him." My stomach twists. I still feel nervous telling her when I'm doing stuff with Cooper even if we don't have plans.

"You spent most of last weekend with him making that stupid video."

"It was for Superman," I say.

She keeps going. "And you were with him when you were supposed to be with me at the dance." She floats on her back, her face to the sky. "Can't you do whatever you're doing with him another day?"

"No, but—" She interrupts me before I can ask her to join us.

"I don't get why you even hang out with him."

"What do you mean?" I ask, shocked she'd say this. "He's my friend."

"He's weird," she says, diving into a wave.

I stand there stunned. Not diving. Not moving. When she pops back up, I say, "No, he's not."

"He always wears that tan shirt and smells like peanut butter. Or garbage. Or something gross. And eats lunch in the science lab."

"*I* eat lunch in the science lab," I say, my throat dry.

"That's different," she says.

I stare at my friend, not wanting her to be like Mickey Ray when he called me a weirdo in front of everyone in first grade.

And not wanting me to be like the kids who stood there and said nothing.

So I dig deep to find Fearless Fred and say, "I think Cooper's nice. Plus, he loves animals and has a super-cute dog." Then I wriggle my toes deep into the squishy ocean sand and hope my words didn't mess things up.

Logan's quiet.

My insides roll like the waves.

Logan turns to me, tucks her hair behind her right ear, and says, "Whatever. It's up to you if you want to hang out with a weirdo."

Eight Steps

The next morning, the doorbell rings, and before I can answer it, I hear Pickle say, "Hi. You're the one who ran over Superman."

"Yep, that's me," Cooper says. "And thanks to your mom, he's doing okay."

When I walk into the room, Pickle's spinning in her pajamas and cape, and I want to melt into the cranberry-red shag carpet.

I put my hand on Pickle's shoulder, hoping to stop all the twirling. But I'm too late. She falls to the ground, dizzy, laughing.

Thankfully, Cooper laughs too. "I like your cape," he says.

I exhale the embarrassment that comes with having a little sister.

"Thanks." Pickle smiles and stands up. "Will you save me a whoopie pie?"

"Sure," I tell her as she runs off.

"Hey," Cooper says. "I brought the stuff to make the signs." That's part two of our plan. Part one, we bake the whoopie pies. Part two, we make the signs. Part three, we sell the whoopie pies.

"And I have all the ingredients we need. I didn't even have to buy anything. My dad used to bake all the time. One year for my mom's birthday he made chocolate donuts." That's one of my top five days. We were the four of us. Together. With chocolate. It felt like nothing could change us.

Cooper follows me into the kitchen. Which is just eight steps from where we were standing. "My mom told me that Mr. Magoo is doing much better."

"Yep. He's almost back to himself." He lifts his black Converse and points to the quarter-size hole his dog ate in the side.

I'm so happy about this—not the hole he chewed, just that he's improving—but it makes me think about Beautiful You and Super Worried. What if this is connected? The testing. The poison. Mr. Magoo. Mom doesn't know exactly what he got into. He's getting better now. But what if he gets worse again?

I have to ask. Maybe I can help. "I, um, heard about this new company in town, Beautiful You. And, um, I think they may be testing their blush and makeup stuff on animals." I hope this sounds normal.

I wait for him to be outraged. But he's not. He's silent.

"I, um, wonder if you think this could be connected to Mr. Magoo. Like maybe he got into the company's toxic trash."

There, I said it. Then I bite my lip as I set all the ingredients on the counter.

"It's not connected," he says.

His certainty surprises me. I stir the buttermilk and vanilla together in Dad's favorite blue bowl. "Well, hopefully not. But, I, um can help you look into it so we can find out for sure, or I can ask my mom or something. I mean, if you want."

"I don't," he says, mixing the flour, cocoa, baking soda, and salt in a separate dish. "Mr. Magoo was nowhere near there. This is totally unrelated."

"But how do you know? I mean what if it *could* be helpful?" I ask. I grab the electric hand mixer and beat the butter and brown sugar while Cooper scrapes the batter off the sides. When it's fluffy we add the egg and sugar mixture.

"It's not," he says. Then, "Can we drop it?"

I nod, even though I'm not convinced this isn't somehow connected. We put the chocolate cakes in the oven and move on to the creamy inside.

"Look, I know you're just trying to help," he says, adding the marshmallow creme. "Don't mean to be a jerk."

"No worries. I know you can't help it."

We both laugh. Then he says, "I thought maybe we could make some with peanut butter filling." Cooper holds up the jar he brought.

"Sounds good," I say. We dump in a few large scoops to the cream, add a drop of water, and mix.

Then we wait.

This is the hardest part for me. I never know what to do with the silence. It feels like it's screaming for me to fill it, but I don't know how. And I don't want to bring up Beautiful You again.

So I wash the bowls and mixers. Put away the ingredients. Wipe the counters.

I look over at Cooper, who's eating the leftover marshmallow creme and peanut butter.

He offers me a heaping spoonful. It's delicious.

I look around and we still need to wait for the chocolate cakes to finish baking and cool. What are we going to talk about? My brain twists, praying my restless nerves aren't showing.

"This your dad?" Cooper asks, holding a photo of Pickle, me, and Dad at a Red Sox game. That was when he was just Regular Dad with a hot dog.

I nod because the words stick.

"When's he coming back?"

I shrug. Not sure he's even coming back anymore. Last night I deleted from my calendar the date he's supposed to return. "There's a date. But stuff comes up."

"You miss him?"

I nod. I know if I say what my heart is feeling, tears will roll. And I don't want that. Not now. Not here. Not with Cooper.

"I never knew my dad," Cooper says. "So I don't really miss him."

"Oh," I say.

"Do you think it's worse knowing the person who leaves? So you're left missing him?"

I never said I missed my dad.

"Or never knowing him?"

Can he tell just by looking at me that there's an imprint on my heart where my dad used to be?

"I think they're both like eating burnt whoopie pies. Something no one wants," I say.

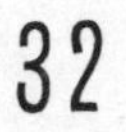

32

Next Time

While the whoopie pies' chocolate goodness cools, Cooper and I make posters for our stand. But my whoopie pie looks more like a big brown spaceship than a delicious dessert. I'm trying to think of a way to fix it when my phone pings. Text from Logan: *Mom bailed early. Can you hang?*

I freeze, not sure what to say. She called Cooper a weirdo, so it's not like I can invite her now.

I text: *Can't today. Sorry :(*

Logan: *?*

Me: *Doing that thing with Cooper. Remember?*

Logan: *?*

Me: *Making whoopie pies*

Logan: *Why?*

Me: *To raise money to pay for stuff for his dog*

Logan: *As I said, weird. But I love whoopie pies*

Me: *I promise to save you one!* 🙂

Logan: *Yay! Want help?*

I bite my nail. I want to invite her. It'd be fun to do this with both my friends. And I was going to invite her.

But then she called Cooper weird and said all that mean stuff. I know she's not really like that, but I can't do that to Cooper. I crack my knuckles and wish having two friends wasn't so confusing.

Me: *Almost done and then my mom needs help at Hillview Vet. Next time.* ❤

Logan: 🙁 👎

I stuff my phone into my pocket, hoping that bending the truth with one friend to save another from hurt is an okay thing to do.

When Cooper and I are done, we have four large signs and forty-eight whoopie pies. I put one pie on a plate for Pickle and save one for Logan. I wrap the rest to take with us. We set up the stand at the corner near Hillview Vet, just outside of Delilah's Flowers. I thought it would be a good spot. Lots of people. But for the first hour it's just hot and slow.

Cooper's sweating and quiet and I wonder if he wishes he recruited someone else to help.

He wipes the sweat dripping down the side of his

face with the back of his hand. "When it's hot like this, it reminds me of D.C. in the summer," he says.

"Do you miss it?"

He shakes his head. "I miss my friends. And I miss that it was, you know, what I was used to. But it was hard there, too."

"How?" I ask, hoping that sounds normal.

"My mom was out of work for a long time. Didn't really have our own place. Stayed on friends' couches a lot."

"What about family?"

He shakes his head. "I didn't know. It must have been hard not having a home."

He shrugs. "I've never thought of home as a place. More like wherever I am with my mom."

I look at my friend. Maybe he's right. Maybe my forever home isn't a house with lilac bushes, but wherever I am with Mom and Pickle. And maybe Dad.

"I get that," I say. "But I'm sorry it was hard for you."

He takes a swig from his water bottle. "It's cool. My mom has a job now. And I have Mr. Magoo." He smiles.

Before I can say anything else, the Braves soccer team walks up to our stand with a guy who introduces himself as Coach Manchel. Practice just wrapped up. I count seventeen players and two other coaches. And they're hungry. Twenty whoopie pies sold. Cooper smiles and starts talking to one of the kids about their scrimmage. Turns out they won, four to two.

Mr. and Mrs. Brownstein are out for a walk and buy ten, one for each grandson. "Our daughter's pregnant again, and this time I'm secretly hoping for a girl," Mrs. Brownstein tells me with a wink. I wrap up her whoopie pies and put extra napkins in the bag.

A woman walking two Labrador retrievers and a beagle, a guy with a dozen roses from Delilah's, and a family of five all stop for whoopie pies. Ten more gone. The guy with the roses eats three right there. "I eat when I'm nervous," he says. "I'm about to propose."

"Wow. Good luck," Cooper says.

Then kindergarten after-school comes by. The kids are holding hands. A woman who introduces herself as Mrs. Fischer is at the front of the line. She buys the rest of the whoopie pies. The kindergartners cheer.

"I can't believe it," Cooper says. "We did it. We sold them all." He reaches down, counts the money, splits it, and gives me half.

I shake my head. "I don't want it. We did this for you and Mr. Magoo."

"But you earned it."

"I didn't do it for that," I say, grabbing the posters. "I did it to help. Just use the money to take care of Mr. Magoo."

He puts the cash in his pocket. “Next time let’s make a bunch of other flavors. Like mint chip and caramel and sea salt.”

I smile.

I guess there will be a next time.

33
Freaking Out

I can't sleep. *The Express* comes out tomorrow with the new secret voice of Dear Student. I try counting backward from one hundred. Take deep breaths. I even listen to a sleep story about iguanas on my phone. Nothing helps. My mind stacks with worry bricks.

Maybe I should never have said yes to Mr. Baker.

Maybe no one will like my advice.

Maybe everyone will know it's me.

Then no one will like me.

The sweat trickles down the back of my neck, tracing my nerves as they bounce across my body.

I flip my pillow. Tuck and untuck my favorite blanket.

But I can't quiet my worries. Finally, when the sun comes up, I get out of bed quietly so I don't wake Pickle.

I toss on my Sea World T-shirt, skip breakfast, and when I open the doors of Hillview Middle, I see Jules reading the paper and laughing with Maya and Evie.

Are they laughing at me? I hold my breath as I walk past them.

Do they know I'm the secret voice?

Then I hear Jules say something about her little brother running naked through the house because he didn't want a moth to eat his clothes, and I exhale.

This is not about me.

On my way into class, I bump into Juan. "You #teamapple or #teampumpkin?"

"What are you talking about?" I ask.

"Check it out." Juan shows me his phone with *my* Dear Student response.

A sprig of happiness shoots from my rainbow-striped socks.

"Mr. Baker said the winner's going to be the dessert for Pi Day in the spring," he says quickly before he slides into his chair.

Maybe I *can* do this.

I take out last night's assignment. Mr. Baker has us read from our stories. Evie goes first. She stands and shares about a girl and her dog named Blue who are inseparable until one day he goes missing.

I stare at the empty chair two away from me. Logan texted she'll be late today. Something about a pimple she's freaking out about. I cross my fingers, hoping that if she's reading the paper, she likes the advice Super Worried got from Dear Student—and never finds out it came from me.

Mr. Baker nods in my direction. It's my turn. I wipe my sweaty hands on my jeans and wish Mr. Baker would let me pass my story around without having to actually read it out loud. That's my least favorite part. But today I do something different. I stand as I read more about Kiko and Apollo.

> *The boy with the mean dad was picking on Max again. At first, she saw only Max's favorite green ninja backpack in the pricker bush by the house where the dog who barked a lot lived. Then she heard angry words and crying. Max needed her help.*
>
> *But Kiko knew in that place that didn't lie that Max had broken his promise. Had told her secret and was the reason her powers of invisibility were gone.*

She walked past the ninja backpack. Then stopped, turned around, and walked back toward the pricker bush.

By the time we go around the room, I hear about a robot who farts, a girl who only wants to eat green food, a boy who climbs to the top of a mountain where Greek gods live, a kid who trades licorice to save his friend from an underground world of magic, and a golden flower that never dies.

The rest of the morning drags. I braid and unbraid and braid my hair again. In history, Ms. Eisner catches me doodling while she's talking about Mesopotamia. But I can't focus. My brain feels twitchy. I haven't seen Logan yet and need to know what she thinks about the advice she got from Dear Student. The advice she got from me.

When class ends, I dart to my locker and hold my breath. Partly because I pass a kid who used way too much body spray and partly because Logan's walking toward me.

She's wearing new pink glasses and reading the paper out loud.

My throat burns.

She reads the headlines from the front page, the opinion piece about whether Hillview Middle School should get uniforms, and stops at the Dear Student letters.

I act like I'm not freaking out inside and pretend to be interested in Jules and Maya and Evie's breakdown of their trip to the Brighten Valley Mall.

"The perfect jeans are so hard to find," Maya says, slamming her locker door.

I search for my Spanish book in my locker, waiting for Logan to say something about the new voice of Dear Student.

"The last two pairs I bought I had to return the next day," Jules says.

Then Logan stops reading and slides her phone into her pocket.

This is it.

The moment when I find out what she thinks. About the advice. Dear Student. And me.

"Have you guys tried that new store next to Gordon Books?" Logan asks. "Janice said they have amazing stuff."

What? Shopping? Really?

Nothing about the email. Nothing about Dear Student.

I grab my notebook while a giant sense of dread crashes over me.

Logan hates the advice. My advice.

She knows it's me.

She hates my advice *and* knows it's me.

Logan hates me.

34

All My Fault

The bell sounds and I bolt like lightning down the hall. I don't know why I ever thought I could do this. I'm relieved when I get to Spanish that Logan takes Mandarin. Señora López has us pair with a partner to practice conjugating the verbs on our list. Cooper walks over to my desk and smiles. I guess we're partners. He's wearing his favorite tan shirt. I can't tell if he has lots of these or just one that he wears all the time. Either way, it's clear he also doesn't know anything about the perfect jeans. Which makes me feel a bit better.

When we're done conjugating "I/you/we/they go to a zombie movie" in Spanish—*Voy a la pelicula zombie. Él va a la película zombie. Vamos a la pelicula zombie. Ellos van a la película zombie*—we go on to the other verbs on the list.

Cooper moves closer. "Thanks again for doing the whole whoopie pie thing," he whispers in English. Then he pulls out *The Express,* reads the opinion piece about changing the dress code, and tells me that he hates the idea of uniforms.

"I mean, how can they expect people to buy all new clothes?"

I hadn't ever thought about it like that. I look down at my orange orangutan shirt. I assumed a dress code would just stop things like the perfect-jean discussion and make it easier for people like me who own mostly animal T-shirts.

Then he turns to the Dear Student letters and my heart pounds.

Loud and furious.

I want to know what he thinks about Dear Student. But mostly I want him to like the advice I gave.

"And this." He points to Logan's letter. "I love animals too, but this is dumb."

Right now I want a giant space vacuum to extract me and drop me into a vortex.

"That Dear Student person wants to protest and shut down this company," he says, his face turning red.

That Dear Student person.

"What's wrong with people!"

His English-speaking voice is raised and Señora looks over. "*Español, por favor,* Cooper."

Spanish ends in a blur.

I run out of class, but Cooper follows me. "Do you think they even considered that maybe this company is doing a good thing opening here?" His angry words fly into the hall.

I stop running and turn around. "I don't get you," I say, confused. "You have a dog and love animals. So how can you think a company that experiments on innocent animals like Spud is doing anything good?"

"Jobs! The company's creating jobs. You know, for people who need them so they can eat and live."

Oh.

"I get that Super Worried and Dear Student care about animals. But I don't get why they don't care about people." His voice is a mix of serious and sad.

"That's not fair," I say.

"What's not fair is that all the people who work at Beautiful You will lose their jobs if the company is forced to shut down."

I stare at him.

"How do you know that's the company they're even talking about?" The Dear Student letter doesn't mention a name.

"It's the only one that's moved into town recently. The only one offering lots of jobs. But now, thanks to that Dear Student person and Super Worried, those jobs could be gone tomorrow." He pauses. "And people like my mom will once again be unemployed."

"That's where your mom works?" I ask, staring at him.

He nods. "That's the job we moved here for. The one that took her over a year to find."

I swallow. "I didn't know."

He stuffs his books into his backpack and turns around to me. "It's not your fault that Super Worried and that Dear Student person want to shut down Beautiful You."

But as he walks away, I know he's wrong.

It's all my fault.

35

A Secret

I don't want Cooper's mom to lose her job. I don't want anyone to lose their job. I just want animals to be safe.

Why do I have to choose?

I speed-walk down the hall to find Mr. Baker. I need to know how to fix this. I take the back stairs to avoid as many people as possible.

I pop out of the hall and unfortunately run right into Logan.

"Great. I have to talk to you," she says, taking my hand.

"Can we please do this later? I have to go to the bathroom," I say to her sparkly sneakers. I know this isn't exactly true, but my nerves are making me feel like my body's on fire from the inside. So splashing cold water on my face isn't such a bad idea. Plus, I don't want to mention Mr. Baker and I really don't want to talk before I can figure out how to fix this.

Logan ignores my words and pulls me into the rear stairwell. We tuck into the space under the stairs, which is covered with dog stickers.

She leans in. I can smell her sour-lemon-candy breath. "Can I tell you a secret?"

I nod.

"I'm Super Worried!"

"That makes two of us. I'm superworried also." I feel the nerves zip and fizzle across my stomach.

"No. I mean I *am* Super Worried. You know, the person who wrote to Dear Student!"

My mouth is dry as dust and my heart pounds like it did the time I ran a 5K with Mom to raise money for endangered sea turtles. Except I'm not running. I'm standing in a stairwell that smells like the cafeteria's version of pizza, staring at a poodle sticker.

What am I supposed to do now? Tell Logan that I know she's Super Worried because I'm actually Dear Student?

She looks around to make sure no one's coming down the steps. When she sees we're alone she starts talking again. "I wrote to the secret advice columnist about that cosmetics company I told you about, and they wrote back."

Is omission the same as lying?

"And I got the best advice!" she says.

What?!

"We're going to organize a march. It was actually something I thought about even before Dear Student's advice, but I worried it was maybe, you know, too much or dumb."

I didn't know Logan worried about that kind of stuff.

"But now, I'm sure it's the right thing to do. I'm going to call it KAT—Kids Against Testing," she says in her save-the-world voice.

Uh-oh.

"And we're going to stop the company from opening here and save the animals."

"We?"

She squeezes my hands. "Please say you'll do this with me. I'm going to recruit my mom, Zahara, the Your Voice Matters Club, and I thought maybe you could talk to your mom and ask her to join the fight."

I stare at my friend with her got-things-to-do excitement. I want to say testing on animals is a million times wrong. I want to say I'd do anything to protect the Spuds of the world. I want to say there's no mascara, blush, or eye shadow that makes this okay. But "Maybe" is all I spit out.

The rest of my words are stuck behind the mound of confusion that comes from hurting someone I care about by doing something I believe in.

"Autumn, no one wants this company in business."

But I know she's wrong.

I can think of one very angry boy with a buzz cut and a blue bike who does.

A Bundle of Confusion

I should be happy.

Logan likes my advice.

But I'm not.

I'm a bundle of confusion. I have two friends who want something different. Something opposite. The friend who doesn't know that I know that she asked me for advice is taking the advice I gave. But the other friend who doesn't know that I'm the one giving advice is mad about the advice I gave.

At this point, I'd be happier if they both hated my advice. At least they'd be in agreement.

What am I supposed to do now?

I text Prisha. She doesn't respond. I look at the time. She's still at school.

I flop onto my bed with my stuffed platypus, Pepper, and Spud.

"Why does everything with humans have to be so hard?" I ask, rubbing the *hamsa* around my neck.

Spud munches on a cucumber peel.

"And complicated?"

More cucumber peels.

I jump online for answers, not sure what exactly I'm looking for. So I end up watching videos about oddly paired pets—like a kangaroo hugging a monkey, a dog with a bunch of ducklings, and a cat playing with a chinchilla.

"I don't know what to do," I say to Spud, who's climbing across my lap.

"About what?" It's Pickle.

"You need to knock when our door's closed," I say. This is the rule even now that we share a room. Door closed means private space.

"I did knock," she says. "Well, not really, but I thought about it. Then I heard you say you didn't know what to do, so I came to help."

I tilt my head and stare at my sister with the lime-green cape, striped tights, and hair that smells like strawberry. "How are you going to help?"

She scoots over to her side of the room. Rummages under her bed and pulls out the once-empty birthday jar that's now filled with lots of little pieces of colored paper. "Here." She hands me the jar. "I'll share it with you so you can figure out what to do."

My eyes sting, grateful for my little sister's superpowers.

I grab the notepad from the top of the honey-colored wooden desk that was Dad's. Sometimes I run my fingertip along the nicks in the wood, wondering if they're from him. I tear off two sheets of paper and give one to Pickle and I take one. Pickle starts drawing a picture. I stare at the blank white page.

What do I want?

I want Logan to save the animals.

I want Cooper to *want* to save the animals.

And I want neither to be mad at Dear Student.

Or at me.

37

Miss You Back

After I put my wishes in the jar, I walk Pickle to Ryan's house. Pickle says she doesn't mind that he doesn't say much because she thinks his quiet is his superpower. When we get to the brick house, Ryan's mom meets us at the door. Pickle runs off with her friend, and I head back toward home and Hillview Vet. Mom asked me to help out. And I've decided it's easier to spend time with Wilbur and Flame and Sugar than with any of my human friends.

I walk through the yellow front door and Bear greets me with a sloppy kiss. I rub his furry body, grateful for his not-confusing-at-all friendship. I give him a cheese-flavored treat, which he hides under his dog bed.

"You look like you're carrying the weight of the world on them shoulders," Malcolm says to me.

I don't agree. But don't disagree either.

His eyes go all serious and he nods like he knows stuff. "Humans or animals, what's the category?" he asks.

"Always humans," I say. "Animals are way easier."

"Want to talk about it?"

I shake my head. I can't. Not yet.

"Okay. If you change your mind, you know where to find me." He smiles.

I kiss Bear's nose. "I'll be back," I call to Malcolm as I walk away. I promised Mom I'd feed the animals and water the plants. Bear follows me with his squeaky rabbit toy dangling from his mouth. When we get to Superman's cage, I toss Bear the toy and watch him run after it down the hall. Then I give Superman his favorite dandelion leaves.

My phone pings. Text from Logan: *Want to hang out? Figure out march stuff?*

I look at Superman. "I'm glad you're a reptile."

I text Logan back: *Can't today. Helping my mom at Hillview Vet*

"What do you think I should do about the confusing humans?" I ask Superman. He stares at me and chews the greens.

"Should I tell Logan that I'm Dear Student?" I toss in some kale. "If I tell her my secret now, I'm worried she'll be mad I didn't tell her before. But if I say nothing, then I have to pretend I don't know she wrote to Dear Student. That I don't know she's Super Worried." Superman bobs his head up and down. "And Cooper's so mad at Dear Student, and me."

My iguana friend finishes his green leafy treat.

I wipe my eyes that brim with uncertainty. Bear's nails tap on the tile floor behind me. I turn around to toss him his toy again. But it's not Bear. It's Mr. Magoo and Cooper. Walking right toward me.

I bite my lip, wishing there was a place to hide. I don't want to hear about *that Dear Student person* anymore.

But there's no way to disappear. Mr. Magoo comes over and licks my cheek.

"He just had his follow-up visit. Your mom said he's all good," Cooper says, running his hands through his buzz cut.

"Glad he's better," I say.

"Yeah. Me too."

"Did my mom ever figure out what he got into?" I ask, rubbing Mr. Magoo's chin.

Cooper nods. "She thinks maybe some mushroom or mold he ate by accident." He looks at me. "It had nothing to do with Beautiful You."

"Oh," I say in a quiet voice filled with sorry. "I'm just happy he's better."

When I leave Hillview Vet, Prisha calls. I tell her about Cooper and Logan and Beautiful You.

"It's so confusing," I say. "Logan doesn't seem to like Cooper. And the things they want are opposite. No matter what I do, someone's going to be hurt or mad." I sigh. "I've messed up everything. I don't know why there's any part of me that thought I could do this."

"You don't have to stay the voice of Dear Student if you don't want to do it anymore," Prisha says. "Remember when we were in fourth grade and I quit ballet?"

"Yeah. You were supposed to be my partner at our performance. Instead I had to partner with pink-hair, pointy-eyebrow Ms. Sharon. I think that may be why I hate to dance now."

Prisha laughs. I miss her laugh. "Yeah, sorry about that." Then she says, "Look, Autumn, if you don't want to do this thing, don't do it. But don't bail because you think you're not good at it. Not brave enough. Or your new friends will be mad. Just do you. Whatever that is."

"Miss you," I say.

"Miss you back."

A Really Good Thing

When I find Mr. Baker, he's sitting in his empty classroom at his desk, drinking coffee from a large purple mug.

"Good morning. I was just about to send you a few more Dear Student emails," he whispers.

"Yeah, about that." I wonder if he can read the banner scrolling across my brain that's screaming *You picked wrong!*

His right eyebrow shoots up.

"I don't think this is working," I say, looking just past him at the poster on the wall that says VOTE 4 LEO.

Mr. Baker says nothing, but his left eyebrow slides up to meet the other one.

“I mean, I’m pretty sure I’m exactly the wrong person to give advice.” I clench my hands into tiny balls. “You need someone who knows stuff and gets people, and that’s not me. Unless the stuff people want to know is about dogs or guinea pigs or bearded dragons.” I pause. “But it isn’t. I shouldn’t have applied.” I shouldn’t have seized the day. This shouldn’t be my one thing.

“Interesting. Because there’s been a lot of interest in your responses.”

“That’s kind of the problem. I think someone, a friend-kind-of someone, is mad at me. Well, mad at Dear Student.”

He strokes his beard. “Autumn, I didn’t give you this job because I wanted your opinions to make everyone happy.”

“Good, ’cause that’s definitely not happening,” I say, looking at the next poster in line, A VOTE FOR AVRA IS A VOTE FOR ALL. AND A VOTE FOR ICE CREAM AT LUNCH. Kind of think she might win.

“The truth is, no person or piece of advice will make everyone happy. It’s not possible. The best you can do is be yourself, share honestly from your heart, and hope people will listen. They don’t have to agree.”

“Oh.” I never thought about it like that.

“I still believe you’re exactly the right person for this

job. But if you don't, that's okay. It's most important that you stay true to yourself."

I wonder if he's been talking to Prisha.

"Let's hold off on making the decision today. After all, it's Surprise Friday." He smiles.

"What's that?"

"The day I surprise our class with something fun."

"What is it?" I ask.

"Well, if I told you, that wouldn't be a very good surprise," he says, laughing.

Turns out Mr. Baker's Friday surprise was pizza with extra cheese for the entire class, and a movie. We watched the beginning of *Back to the Future* and the weekend assignment was to finish watching and share our thoughts on do-overs and time travel.

I loved my pizza slices and the movie, but my mind was stuck on what Mr. Baker said. That Dear Student isn't about making everyone happy, but about me being me. And getting people to listen.

I remember in second grade telling my teacher Mr. Kellogg, who ate canned peaches for breakfast at his desk every morning, that it wasn't fair that our class celebrated Christmas and not Hanukkah. I loved the Christmas lights and all the traditions, but I also loved the Hanukkah ones I celebrated with my family. But I wasn't superhero-brave then, either. I didn't walk up and tell him. Instead, I wrote him a note on my favorite pumpkin stationery. When Mr. Kellogg read the note, he mumbled something about school policy. But later he invited me and my dad to bring in a menorah and share with the class on the first night of Hanukkah. I remember that day. It's one of my favorites. Not the talking in front of the class; I hated that even then. But bringing in the dinosaur menorah with my dad.

After I get home, I'm still trying to figure out if I should stay Dear Student, when the doorbell rings. It's Logan. Sparkly sneakers. Pink glasses. Aqua skirt. Purple tee. Ponytail.

"Hi," she says, full of sunshine and got-stuff-to-do.

"Hi," I say, searching my brain for a plan that I'm pretty sure we didn't have. "Wait! Did Snow White have her babies?"

Logan shakes her head. "Nope. I'm here to talk to your mom," she says as she moves past me and heads to the kitchen.

I look around. "She's not home yet."

"I know. I just left her downstairs at Hillview Vet. She told me to meet her here because she was almost done for the day."

"Why?" I ask.

"I went to see her about KAT," Logan says, putting a stack of folders on the ugly mauve table that came with our temporary home.

"*You* talked to my mom about the march?"

She nods, taking color-coded paper out of the folders.

My brain feels light and fuzzy like cotton candy. I search for the words I need. "But *I* haven't talked to her about the march yet."

"I assumed you'd told her after we spoke at school the other day."

"I didn't. I mean, I was going to." Maybe. But then Cooper said his mom would lose her job, and that stuck in my heart, and I wasn't sure about the whole march thing anymore.

"I'm sorry," she says. "I thought this was something we both wanted so we could protect animals."

"It is. I mean, I want to protect them. But I'm also worried that if the company closes, all those workers will lose their jobs."

"They'll get other jobs," she says like that's no problem at all. "There are HELP WANTED signs all over the place. I think the real question is, do you or don't you want to be part of the march?"

Before I can answer, the door swings open. "Hey, Autumn. Hi, Logan." It's Mom.

"Thanks for meeting with me," Logan says, moving away from me and toward my mother.

"Sure." Mom pours three glasses of iced tea and opens a box of cider donuts from Millie's Farm.

"I wanted to meet with you to talk about KAT—Kids Against Testing," Logan says, spilling what she's learned about Beautiful You and the animal testing.

My mom gulps down her whole glass. "I read an article about this company in *Today's Veterinarian Journal,*" Mom says. She's always reading. Everything. Like when I got Spud, she told me that she read it's illegal in Switzerland to own just one guinea pig.

"It's terrible. And that's why I came up with the idea to march in protest," Logan says.

You came up with the idea?

"I'm creating KAT—Kids Against Testing—and wonder if you'd support and join the effort to stop animal testing and prevent Beautiful You from opening in Hillview." She gives my mom the color-coded paper, along with printouts of articles and other stuff I can't identify.

The room's quiet. My confusion grows as Mom reads and rereads everything.

Logan watches her. Hands on her hips. Eyes wide. I'm-going-to-do-this expression splashed across her face.

Then Mom clears her throat and turns to me. "Autumn, what do you think?"

All of Me

My body freezes.

My thoughts scramble.

Part of me is impressed with Logan's color-coded confidence.

Part is frustrated she talked to my mom before I did.

All of me is confused.

"I need to use the bathroom," I blurt out, leaving the duo to their donuts and papers, and sprinting to my room. I know that's not an answer to the question. But I need space.

I tuck into my empty room—thankful that Pickle isn't home—sit on my bed and think about my dad. He'd like

Logan. She reminds me of him. A seize-the-day kind of person.

Spud's orange body waddles to the edge of his cage when he sees me. I scoop him up and give him a carrot. His nose twitches as he chomps on his snack. I run my hand down his back. His fur is soft. I stare into his black button eyes and wish he could talk to me.

How can I not do all I can to protect him and all the other Spuds out there? What if Beautiful You experimented on him to find out if blush or eye shadow would cause someone to break out in a gross rash?

Maybe Mr. Baker's right. Maybe Dear Student is about getting people to listen. Really listen to all the ideas.

Maybe it doesn't matter if Cooper's mad.

Or if Logan knows that I'm Dear Student.

Maybe the only thing that matters is that people listen to all of it. The stuff they like and the stuff they don't.

And that I stay true to me.

I run back downstairs. I grab a cider donut, inhale a big breath of I-can-do-this, and say to my mom and my friend, "I've decided I think it's a good idea."

"Thank you!" Logan says, hugging me tight. "I'm going to ask my mom to come too. And Zahara, all the kids from Your Voice Matters, and, well, everyone!"

After Logan leaves, I take out my notebook and write. About orange ribbons and seizing the day and Dad. About things I like and things that scare me.

The time drifts. Before bed there's one more thing I need to do. I take a huge breath of brave before it disappears behind my door and send Mr. Baker an email:

> Mr. Baker,
>
> I've made my decision. I'm going to stay on as the secret voice of Dear Student.
>
> Thanks for believing in me.
>
> ~Autumn

Mr. Baker gets right back to me.

> I'll always believe in you. Just glad you now believe in yourself, too.

Accidentally Ate Brussels Sprouts

The next day, the news about the march is all over Hillview Middle. Seems after the meeting at the apartment last night, Logan texted and called everyone she could think of, telling them that we were marching and asking them to join us. And then those kids told kids who told kids who told kids. At lunch, Jules, Maya, and Evie say they want to be part of KAT. I spy Cooper, but he ignores me or doesn't see me. Either way, he doesn't speak to me.

My heart hurts. I don't want him to be mad. At Dear Student or me. I want him to understand that we're just trying to keep animals safe.

In English, Mr. Baker talks about how marches over the years have impacted our nation. From the famous civil rights march where Martin Luther King Jr. gave his "I Have a Dream" speech to the anti–Vietnam War marches, the Million Man March, and the Women's Marches. He tells us some marches are against action while others are in support of change. And some are both.

"You may not agree with the opposition, but to truly effect change, you need to be respectful and listen." He looks my way for just a second and then moves on. "Change takes conviction, perseverance, commitment, and passion."

I feel like he's reading the message on one of his T-shirts.

Mr. Baker hops off his desk. "At the top of a sheet of paper, I want you to write something that's important to you."

Reilly raises her hand. "Can it be basketball?"

Mr. Baker nods. "It can be anything you feel passionate about."

"Like protecting mice and pigs and dogs from experimental testing," Amar says, turning toward me and smiling.

"And women's rights," Rena shares.

"And more care packages for our military," Xavier

says. His mom's in the Army and is recently back from being deployed in Afghanistan. Over the summer, he organized a send-care-packages-to-the-troops block party. We sent soap and books and our neighbor's amazing homemade chocolate chip cookies.

"After you write what you're passionate about at the top, on the left side of the paper write all the reasons you support this cause. On the right side, put down all the reasons someone might be against this cause."

At the top of my paper I write *KAT*.

REASONS FOR KAT

We have to protect all animals.

It's important to fight for people and animals who don't have a voice and can't fight for themselves.

Don't ignore stuff just because it doesn't harm you personally.

REASONS AGAINST KAT

The company creates jobs. If the company closes, jobs will be lost.

Testing prevents people from getting gross rashes.

I can't think of anything else to include in either column. It looks almost even, which is confusing. Because it isn't. Because experimenting on innocent animals is never okay.

"Now, turn to the person sitting to your left and make the case *against* your cause," Mr. Baker says as he walks around the desks.

Groans stretch across the classroom.

"Knowing the opposition's position will enable you to strengthen your own claims."

Markus Bell is to my left. His cause is no homework over the weekends. But now he has to argue in favor of homework, which seems wrong no matter what you're passionate about.

When it's my turn, I need to argue in favor of experimenting on helpless, trusting, innocent animals. Which also feels wrong. But I think of Cooper and argue for jobs. Then I think of Reggie, who said his face would blow up like a balloon if he ate shrimp, and argue the importance of testing on animals instead of people even though in my heart I don't think you should test on either. I believe with all the science and new technology, there has to be another way. A better way. And even though I don't want to be, Markus tells me I'm convincing.

After English, I see Cooper at his locker. Maybe he

didn't see me this morning or was just in a bad mood about something completely unrelated to me. Like he accidentally ate brussels sprouts or missed the bus. Mom always says not to assume someone's bad mood is your fault.

I walk right up to him. Like he's not mad at me.

"Hey," I say, noticing that his favorite tan shirt has a small hole in the bottom left corner.

He looks at me, nods, then slams his locker and walks away.

I'm not sure what to do now. We're actually both heading to Spanish, but it feels awkward to trail him there. So I wait until I see him turn the corner and then walk to Spanish alone.

When I get there, Señora greets me with, "Hola, Otoño."

"Hola, Señora." Her dark hair is tucked into a green beret and her moon necklace shimmers when she moves. I wonder if it belonged to someone before her. Like my *hamsa*.

I find my seat next to Cooper. His back is to me and he doesn't shift or move or say hi when I sit down. I'm starting to think Mom may be wrong.

We discuss in Spanish our homework from last night. I doodle *Kids Against Testing* in my notebook. Cooper glances at me and then looks away when I turn toward him. After class, I decide talking to him is not a good idea. I grab my books, but when I get up to leave, he's next to me.

"I can't believe you're organizing this stupid march. You know, the one that Dear Student person suggested?"

There it is again. *That Dear Student person.*

"I'm not organizing it. I'm supporting it."

I'm not sure how exactly he found out, but at this point in the day, it seems the entire school knows about it.

"Same thing," he says in a low, grumbly voice.

"Not really." Organizing is all about color-coded paper and talking to lots of people. But I don't say that. "I know how much you care about animals. And I think if you knew more about what the company was doing, you'd support the march too. I mean, think about Mr. Magoo and how he almost died the other night. What if that happens again? On purpose?"

"You don't get it," he says with eyes full of anger.

"I know. You told me about the job thing and I get that's hard. Especially since that's why you moved here."

He shoves his hands in his pockets.

"But I've been thinking about that. And maybe I can help make a list or something. There are lots of other jobs your mom can get." Just like what Logan said. "At Food Mart or Dezzi's Diner or Dr. Abrams's dentist office—Pickle was just there for a cleaning and there was a big HELP WANTED sign for a dental hygienist. Or Shoe Barn or Damion Sports World or—"

"Like I said, you don't get it." He turns and walks away again. But this time, I know he's mad at me.

And at *that Dear Student person.*

41

The Next Big Thing

At home, I slump into my beanbag chair, grab my notebook, and write at the top:

How do I choose?

What's the right thing to do when both sides of something have good stuff and bad stuff? When no matter what I do, some person or animal I care about will get hurt?

I thought I had it figured out. What mattered. To me. I thought I knew. But now that's scattered again in my mind and my heart. I wait for Fearless Fred to show up and tell me the answers. But he doesn't.

My phone rings. It's Logan. She rattles off all the

other people she's reached out to about KAT. "And the best part," she says, "is my mom and dad promised we'd march together."

"That's great," I say in a worry-coated voice.

"What's wrong?" she asks.

I take in a deep breath. "I'm not sure I can march."

"What do you mean? We're doing this together." I hear the anger wedge between her words.

"I mean, I'm not *not* doing it. But I'm not one hundred percent sure I am doing it." I bite the end of the pencil I'm holding.

"I don't get you," she says. "I thought you were all in."

She sighs really loudly and my brain fogs. "I was. But then I talked to Cooper again and now my feelings are all mixed up."

"What about Spud? Wouldn't you feel bad if someone experimented on him?"

"Of course! I'd do anything to protect him."

"Then do it. You actually have a chance to make a difference," she says.

"But I'm worried about Cooper and his mom."

"Stop worrying all the time," she says. "Just do what you know is right."

I'm trying.

"Look, I've got to go." Logan pauses and clears her throat like my mom does when she tells me something she knows I'm not going to want to hear. "Autumn, I'm doing this march with or without you."

"I know," I say, and bite my lip as a sliver of sad slips into my heart.

"But I hope it's with you." She hangs up the phone.

I'm staring at the almost-empty page in my notebook when Mom sits down next to me. I lean in. Her sweatshirt smells like the campfire we made the last time she wore it.

I tell her about my conversations with Logan and Cooper, and then tell her about the jobs and Beautiful You. "I'm so confused. How do I march knowing it could hurt Cooper and his family?" I sigh. "But how do I not do all I can to protect and save the animals?"

Mom wipes the tears rolling down my cheek.

"Why does it have to be so hard? Why can't helping just be the right thing to do?" I ask, twirling the rogue piece of hair that's fallen out of my braid.

"It is. But when you care about both sides of something, it can also feel complicated."

"And really confusing. And kind of sad."

"When fighting for something you believe in, you have to stay true to yourself and focus on the part you can control." She holds my hands.

"Like with Dad."

She nods.

"I'm worried he's never coming home," I say. Then I take in all the courage I can find and ask, "Is he?"

"He says he is," she says.

"Do you believe him?" I ask.

I've thought about this a lot. At what point do you stop believing someone who tells you the truth you want so badly to hear? Is it the first time they don't do what they say? Or the second? Or the tenth? Or do you want their words to be true so badly that you decide to believe them forever?

"I have to," she says, wiping away her own tears.

"Sometimes I'm really mad at him."

"It's okay to be mad. It's okay to feel all the things you're feeling. His decision to leave was confusing. It was a hard decision to make, but it also took courage."

"Stop saying that. I think it would have been way braver to stay."

She kisses the top of my head.

We don't talk for a bit. I hear the thump of the dryer spinning in the other room.

"My brain feels kind of like our broken dryer. Twisted and thumping. I can't figure out what I should do."

"Autumn, do you believe the cosmetics company's testing on animals is wrong?"

"Yes." I look at my mom. Her brown hair has streaks of gray that I've never noticed before.

"Do you believe you can effect change in a different way?"

"No. I mean, Logan already tried writing a letter and the company ignored it."

Mom's dark brown eyes are warm and full of love. "Stand behind your beliefs. Your friends may not agree with you, but they'll respect you for standing up for something that matters to you."

I hope so.

But I'm not totally sure.

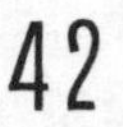

42

Fight for Us

I think about what Logan said and what Mom said. But mostly I think about what I want. Then I call Logan and tell her that I'm marching. That I want to do what I can to protect Spud. And to stand up for animals that can't stand up for themselves.

Today we're meeting at Hillview Vet to make signs for the march. It's one week away. And when I walk downstairs with Mom and Pickle, my eyes get big. The sidewalk is bumping-into-people packed. I look for Cooper, but he's not here. I didn't really think he'd come, but I invited him anyway and hoped he'd change his mind. I want him to want to be a part of this. And I want him not to be mad at me.

Someone taps my shoulder. I turn around and spy Evie, Maya, and Jules, all the kids from Your Voice Matters, Logan, and lots more kids I've seen in the halls at school. I count but lose track at around forty-eight.

I snap a pic and send it to Dad.

Part habit.

Part wanting him to be proud of this.

Of me.

Because what he thinks matters to me. Even if I don't want it to.

He texts back: *Way to seize the day!*

"Look at all these people who came for KAT!" Logan says, jumping up and down in her sparkly sneakers.

I'm happy that so many people want to protect animals like Spud. But I'm also kind of overwhelmed. This feels like a lot. Of everything. I wonder if that's what brave feels like.

Mom opens the yellow door and everyone pours in. Logan hands out poster board and different color markers. I slide into a corner and make a sign with a picture of Spud—or a guinea pig that's orange and supposed to look like Spud—and it says KIDS AGAINST TESTING: PROTECT OUR PETS in orange marker. Logan's working on one with a beagle on the front and STOP ANIMAL TESTING written in big letters on the back.

Pickle's poster has a giant bunny face with a heart around it.

"Is your mom joining us today?" Mom asks Logan. "I'm ordering pizza for all the volunteers."

"No. She's working." She pushes back her blue suede headband.

I look over at her and wonder if she's stuffed away her disappointment like I do with Dad. After I told her I was a go for the march last night, she said she was excited because her mom was joining us to make signs. But when I texted this morning, she sent me a sad face emoji next to the words: *An important meeting came up. My mom can't make it* And before I could respond, she sent me a second text: *Totally get it though. Someone has to fight for us* ♥

I look at her now and know that's true. But understanding that something is important doesn't make it hurt less.

I should know.

"You okay?" I slide next to Logan and help her color in the green background of the poster she's working on.

She nods.

"Sorry about your mom."

She nods again and says, "You get it. I mean, it's the same with your dad."

I so wish that wasn't true.

But it is. My dad and her mom really aren't that different. They're both saving the world and leaving behind the ones who love them most.

Over the next few hours, we make sixty signs and finish eight large pizzas. We decide we will meet at eight a.m. next Sunday at Landings Park, peacefully march down Main Street, and end up across from Beautiful You.

The day is filled with so many humans standing up for my furry and scaled friends. It's kind of weird seeing these worlds come together, but also kind of nice.

Until Logan screams. Loudly.

43

Super Snake

Logan got a text from Mrs. Yard with a photo. Snow White's laying her eggs. "I need to get back," Logan says, grabbing her coat.

I find Mom, who looks at the photo and reassures Logan there's nothing to worry about. Snow White is okay, but Logan still wants to go home.

Once the meeting wraps up, Mom and I drive Logan back while she texts her mom an update about Snow White.

No response.

Then she sends her another text about KAT.

No response.

"I'm sure she's still in that meeting," I say, hoping I

sound more certain than I feel. "Why don't you let your dad know about Snow White? I bet he'll be excited." Her dad's like Logan. Filled with sunshine and big ideas. Today he's pitching his Cricket Chips to some company in Boston.

When we pull in to the driveway, Mrs. Yard's standing in the doorway with a pale face. "Honestly, I agreed to watch you as a favor to your parents. No one said anything about a snake. Much less a pregnant one," she says. "I prefer goldfish." She steps out of the way as we walk inside.

Mom does an initial evaluation of Snow White. "She's doing great," Mom says.

I peek in. It's beautiful. There are four white eggs. They kind of look like chicken eggs, just twice as long.

Before we leave, Mom reminds Logan the eggs will hatch in about sixty days, and until then they'll need to be removed and placed in an incubator. "If you need help, let me know."

We wave goodbye to Mrs. Yard, who's sitting on the sofa eating a giant chocolate bar with whipped cream. "This calms me down when I'm feeling overwhelmed," she says.

Mom smiles.

I tell Logan to text me later.

Pickle gets home just after we do. She hands me two

oatmeal chocolate chip cookies. Turns out, Ryan may not talk much, but he loves to bake, and he and his mom dropped off a dozen delicious cookies to Hillview Vet after we left.

I show her a photo of Snow White and the eggs.

"Can we keep one of the babies?" she asks Mom.

"No baby ball pythons are going to live in this apartment," Mom says. "But maybe we can keep one downstairs."

"I'm going to name her Super Snake," Pickle says, spinning in circles. "And make her a purple cape."

Pickle stops spinning and flops down onto the couch next to me. We read and do homework as Mom darts around the kitchen making lemon-garlic chicken while listening to the news.

Somewhere between wafts of lemon, I hear the TV broadcaster say, "And, in other news, we've learned the students at Hillview Middle School aren't happy about Beautiful You, the cosmetics company, opening its doors in town." I recognize that voice. It's Barry Grayson. He brings his ferret, Mozart, to Hillview Vet. And he's the voice of the local news.

I stop reading.

Pickle's eyes grow wide.

Mom stops cooking and turns up the volume.

"Logan Bellingham and Autumn Blake from Hillview

Middle School have organized a march called KAT—Kids Against Testing, demanding Beautiful You not open unless and until the company agrees to stop testing their products on animals."

"You guys made the news!" Mom says.

"You're famous!" Pickle says.

The broadcaster continues. "We've reached out to Beautiful You for comment but have yet to hear back. Gotta love the passion and tenacity in these kids. Now, on to sports."

All the Missing

On Monday, the entire school is buzzing about the news story. JJ Ray, who has only spoken to me once to ask me to move out of his way, high-fives me in the hall. Zahara tells me I'm an honorary member of the Your Voice Matters Club, and Reilly hands me pins she made with pictures of hearts and animals.

Then this morning before school, Dad video called.

I wasn't sure I even wanted to take it. But I couldn't not. So I jumped on the call and when I saw his big green eyes, all the missing landed in my heart.

"I'm excited about the march, Autumn. Seems you found Fearless Fred."

"Thanks," I said, already knowing that's not enough to bring him home.

"You're a brave one," he said. "Really proud of you."

He went on to tell me about the girls in his host family and the kids at the school and how he feels like he's really making a difference. But that's the confusing part. Because he could be making a difference here.

"Miss you," he said.

"You can't do that," I said, hoping I'm as brave as my dad says I am.

"Do what?"

"Say you miss me. Because if you did—I mean, if you really missed me and Pickle and Mom—you'd come home."

"It's not that simple, Autumn. I made a commitment to the Peace Corps."

"You made a commitment to us. To me. You're my dad. You should be here." That was the last thing I said before the connection cut out.

It felt hard but good to have said at least some of the things that have been turning over and over in my brain. I'm glad he's proud of me. But while he was saying it, I realized that I don't need him to be proud of me anymore. I need him to be home.

During lunch, I go directly to the science lab and sit at the table next to the skeleton. Cooper isn't here.

Which makes me equal parts sad and relieved. But the quiet space feels good. My shoulders unsqueeze and I open my email. More Dear Student letters.

> Dear Student,
>
> Today I heard someone say something really awful to this kid I barely know. I didn't say anything at the time. I mean, he's not my friend. But now I feel like a jerk. What should I do?
>
> Signed,
> Feeling Bad

I breathe in a gulp of peaceful science air. If I can ignite passion—that's what Barry Grayson the broadcaster said on the news—and find Fearless Fred, then maybe I can help Feeling Bad. Honest and heart, those are the two things Baker said make good advice.

> Dear Feeling Bad,
>
> Do something about it. Go up to the kid and apologize. Let him know you've got his back.

I read it over and decide I need to do more. Say more. Seize the day.

Dear Feeling Bad,

I see the pickle you're in, but you need to do something about it. Go up to the kid and apologize. Let him know you've got his back. Say something to the kid who was mean. Whatever you decide, don't do nothing.

It's worse to have people not stand up for you, than for one kid to say something mean. You can ignore the mean thing. But when people start pretending nothing happened, it can make you feel like you don't matter.

It's time to act, my friend.

Signed,
Student

I read it one more time as I take a bite of my bologna and cheese sandwich. When Mickey Ray stood on his chair and called me a weirdo and no one said anything, that hurt more than the words Mickey said. I don't want to write all that. I never really told anyone that part of it. I send this one back to Mr. Baker and open the next email.

Dear Student,

Do you think there's a place or space or thing between dead and alive? I guess the in-between. Where dead people or animals communicate with alive people or animals about stuff that needs fixing?

Sincerely,
Just Curious

I think about Grandma Bea and Grandpa Jack, Rumpelstiltskin and all the stuffed dead animals at Hill-view Vet, and start writing.

Dear Just Curious,

Hmm. Good question with no definitive answer. Likely differs based on your beliefs. For me, I'm a believer in the in-between. Maybe it's because I need to believe that the unsaid and unfinished will have a second chance.

Sincerely,
Student

I eat a gummy frog and open the next email.

Dear Student,

I know a really good person. Like the kind who's trying to make the world a better place. And that's what makes writing this so hard. I'm mad at her. Or maybe just sad. Not sure. She's so busy saving the world that sometimes it feels like she's kind of forgotten about me. Not like in the being-mean way, just in the way she has too many important things to do. It's hard being mad at someone you are related to who is constantly doing good, big things.

I don't have anyone I can ask for help. What should I do?

Sincerely,
Super Worried

The gummy sticks in my throat.

Logan's told me about her mom. And that sometimes it feels bad. But as the lights in the science lab buzz above my head, I realize she's never asked *me* for help. Why? Why does she want advice from Dear Student, but not me?

Either way, I can't let her know that I know.

That's the job.

I also can't let her know that I wish she'd asked me instead of Dear Student.

I think about Logan and her mom. I think about me and my dad. It takes me the rest of my bologna sandwich and all of my gummy frogs to figure out what Dear Student should say to Logan.

> Dear Super Worried,
>
> You can respect someone's hard work and still feel hurt and a little mad. Doing the right thing in the world is important. But so are you and your feelings. So talk to this person. Be honest.
>
> Sincerely,
> Student

I read it, cross my fingers, and hope one day she'll ask me instead of Dear Student.

45 Say Anything

"I thought you were coming over?" Logan says as she walks over to me at the end of the school day.

"I, um, am feeling kind of sick. I'm gonna head home." I grab my backpack and close my locker.

"But I just saw you this morning. You were fine. What happened?"

I got your Dear Student email where you asked her, instead of me, for advice.

"Think I ate something bad at lunch. Maybe it was the bologna," I say.

She makes a face. "My dad says you should never eat processed meats."

"But crickets are okay?"

"I know, that's weird. But he says crickets are natural." Logan smiles. "Seriously, feel better. I'll send you new pics of Snow White when I get home later."

"Thanks."

When I get home, Spud and I zip under my covers, away from everything and everyone.

I text Prisha: *CALL ME! HELP!* And I hug Pepper. I notice he has a new hole under his right arm where the stuffing's coming out.

Thankfully, Prisha has a free block and calls me from the bathroom so she doesn't get in trouble for being on her phone at school.

I love my best friend.

"It was a mistake to do this whole advice thing." I pull my blanket over my head and tell her about how Logan's sad and mad and proud of her mom all at the same time. How she asked Dear Student instead of me for advice. "How do I pretend that I don't know she asked Dear Student for help? And why didn't she just ask me?"

"Look, you can't be jealous of your pseudonym. That's the job, Autumn. And by responding, you're not doing anything wrong."

"But why didn't she ask me for advice? I thought we were friends."

"Don't know. Maybe she was embarrassed or just wanted advice from a stranger. I get that. Sometimes I kind of want to walk up to some random person and tell them what's going on and see what they say."

"Why?"

"Because being anonymous is freeing. You can say anything. Be anyone." She pauses, and I hear a toilet flushing in the background. "I mean, isn't that why you wanted to be Dear Student? Not sure it's really that different."

Maybe Prisha is right. Maybe Logan and I aren't that different.

"I gotta go," she says. "The bell rang for next period and I can't be late for French."

"Thanks. Miss you."

"Miss you back."

I hang up. An hour later, my phone pings. The next edition of Dear Student is out online and I'm happy to be tucked in at home. Logan sends me a text with photos of Snow White and her eggs. I wonder if she's seen Dear Student's advice. Or if she'll ask me for mine. But she doesn't. She just sends more texts of the mama and her eggs. I text back: 🐍🥚👍🙂.

I spend the rest of the afternoon with Mom and Spud and Pickle, not thinking about Dear Student. At night, the worries that pull on my heart weave into my dreams. And when I wake the next day, I decide I'm going to talk to Mr. Baker. This can't be the first time the secret Dear Student got an email asking for advice from a friend.

Logan doesn't text this morning about walking to school together or send a new photo of Snow White and her eggs. Both a little surprising. We've walked to school together most days and there's been a steady stream of snake pics. I text her after weaving my orange ribbon into my braid, but I don't hear back. Mom offers to drive me to school. I don't want to talk about all the stuff that feels confusing, so I focus on slowly eating my blueberry muffin in the truck. Before I pop out at school, she says, "Love you."

I have fifteen minutes before the first bell. Enough time to find Mr. Baker and get help.

When I step into the front hall of the school, a kid in a black knit hat says, "Way to go!"

Before I can figure out what he's talking about, he's already down the hall.

I keep walking.

I turn the corner and see a girl from Spanish who sits in the back row. She looks straight at me. "I totally knew it was you!"

What was me?

I walk faster.

Then someone I don't know says, "Save the planet! Go green!"

I sort of smile, but I'm not sure why this person is talking to me about climate change.

I really need to find Mr. Baker.

When I get to his room, he's sitting at his desk reading something on his computer. He sees me, gets up, and closes the door to his classroom.

That's not good. Mr. Baker has a strict open-door policy.

"I came in early to talk to you." My gaze falls to my high-tops. "About Dear Student stuff. I got an email from someone I know who doesn't know that I'm the secret person and it feels kind of complicated and confusing." Mr. Baker strokes his beard. "But, um . . . there seems to be something else going on." I take a deep breath.

He doesn't say nothing is going on.

He doesn't say everything is fine.

Instead he says, "You're right."

I don't want to be right.

"I feel badly," he says.

I try to use my superpower mind-to-mind reader to figure out what's going on, but the bees in my brain have taken over and all I hear is buzzing.

"I'm not sure how, and I will figure that out, I promise, but—"

"But what?" I ask, desperation leaking out. "What's going on?"

"Somehow your name got out. People know you're the secret voice behind Dear Student."

Like a Wall Between Us

"Autumn, I'm really sorry," Mr. Baker says.

I don't speak. My words are trapped behind stacks of worry. Bricks of confusion. And piles of embarrassment. I shared my truth as Dear Student. Truth I never wanted to share as Autumn Blake. And people shared their truth with me. People like Logan. Truth they never wanted to share with Autumn Blake. And now everyone knows it's me.

I look around. Kids are gathering outside the classroom door. First bell is about to ring. I don't know how I'm supposed to act. Or what I'm supposed to do. All I know is that I need to get out of here. I grab my backpack and bolt out the door, praying I can get to Nurse Kelly's office before anyone else sees me.

But when I move into the hallway, Logan's standing there. She looks different. She's swapped her glasses for contacts and is wearing the sunshine-yellow tee we got together at the beach that day.

I walk over.

She walks away.

"Can I talk to you?" I ask, moving toward her.

"Nope." She keeps walking. "I think you've said enough."

"Please." I follow her.

She spins around. "What do you want?" Her voice is angry.

"I'm sorry," I say.

"Got it." She walks away. Then turns back. "You just better not tell anyone that I wrote in."

I swallow hard. "I won't."

"I asked Dear Student things I didn't want to ask you," Logan says.

"I know. I won't say anything. But just so you know, *we* can talk about that stuff. If you ever, um, want to."

She spins around and starts to leave again.

"You know I couldn't tell you," I say to the back of her yellow shirt.

She stops and turns to look at me. "I know you weren't *supposed* to tell me. But I thought you *would*." She pauses. "Because we're friends. Because I would've told you," she says, her voice coated with sad.

"I'm sorry," I say again. "I wanted to tell you. I did. But *not telling* was one of the things I had to promise."

She exhales the way I do when Pickle tells me something that I don't want to agree with but do anyway. "What I don't get is why you pretended you didn't want to march when KAT was your idea all along?"

"Because I wasn't sure I could," I say. "I'm not like you."

"What does that mean?" Logan asks.

"Brave."

She shakes her head. "I'm not brave, Autumn."

"You're literally one of the bravest people I know. You talk to everyone. You're in, like, a ton of clubs. You aren't scared of anything."

"Being in clubs and talking to people doesn't make me brave. If I was brave, I wouldn't have to ask Dear Student for help. There's lots of stuff that scares me."

How is that possible? I stare at the friend I thought I knew. "Like what?" I ask.

"Being alone," she says.

I think back to Baker's Five Things and remember the thing she hated most. The thing that surprised me.

The doing stuff alone. I guess there are things we never see in people. Even those closest to us.

I hug my brave friend. And she hugs me back.

"You okay?" I ask Logan.

She nods.

"*We* okay?"

She nods again.

The bell rings. Logan dips into class. I head to Nurse Kelly's office.

Down the hall.

Turn the corner.

Cooper's standing there with a new buzz cut. The moment he sees me, I know that he knows. And I know that *we* are not okay.

"I can't believe the march was *your* idea. You were the one who actually started this whole thing," he says.

"I wanted to protect Spud. I told you. I never wanted to hurt you or your mom."

"But you did."

"I'm sorry for that," I say as the hall fills with kids.

"I wish we never moved to this stupid town. I hate everything about this place." The anger in his voice stings.

I search my brain for something helpful to say. To make this better. Or to make him less mad. Or me less sad.

"But you think anyone can just get a job because they want one. Isn't that right, Autumn?"

"I know it's hard. I get that."

Lockers open and close around us.

"You don't know anything. You live in some sort of fantasy world where if you try hard and work hard, everything will just magically be okay."

"I don't think that. But there's another side to this thing. You know, the side where innocent animals get hurt. Or worse."

"You shouldn't be giving advice to anyone." He waits a beat. "You're a fake."

Angry words and hurt feelings stack like a wall between us.

The bell rings.

Cooper walks away.

And I run to Nurse Kelly.

47 A Little Weird

Mom picks me up from school, and when we get home, she flips on the news and makes me chicken soup before she returns to work. Pretty sure she knows I'm not fever-sick or even puke-sick. Just sad-sick. And soup can't fix that, but it tastes good. So that's something.

I give Spud a cucumber peel, pet the soft fur between his ears, and wonder what he'd do if he were me.

He munches the peel and waddles down the ramp in his cage.

"I don't know how to fix this."

"What is it that needs to be fixed?" Mom's back and

is standing at the bedroom door. Hair in a ponytail and shirt covered in fur.

"Me." I rub my *hamsa* charm.

She slides onto my bed next to me. "You don't need fixing." Her hands hold mine. They're soft and warm.

"I can't do anything right. I did this one thing, like Dad asked. I seized the stupid day. Became Dear Student. But really I just made a huge mess of everything."

"You didn't."

"I did. I hurt people I care about," I say, hugging Pepper. "I mean, not on purpose."

"You did the job you were asked to do. You spoke from your heart, and sometimes that's hard and confusing when not everyone shares your truth. But it's also really brave."

"You have to say that; you're my mom." I wipe my cheek and blow my nose. "Cooper hates me. And—" I stop talking.

"What?"

"I'm weird. I mean, I always kind of knew it. I get nervous around new people. I never know what to say and I hate talking in class. But I haven't really felt weird since that time in first grade. At least, not in the bad way." Prisha always says I'm good-weird. Like it's a compliment. I almost believed her. Until today.

Mom looks me in the eyes. "Everyone's a little weird."

I shake my head. "But everyone doesn't *feel* weird."

When Mom leaves, I grab my notebook. I kind of wish I was Kiko. I'd definitely use my invisibility powers. Maybe forever. I write:

Weird
Like a neon yellow crayon
In a sea of pale

Weird
Like a jelly donut
In a box of glazed

Weird
Like a dumbo octopus
In an ocean of fish

Weird
Like me

My tears hit the page, and I feel a tap on my shoulder. It's Pickle, who's excited to tell me that Ryan's mom picked her up from school today with newly dyed hair that's green like Pickle's cape.

Before I can stop the anger bubbling under the surface, I yell, "Get out! The door was closed!"

My little sister starts to cry and races out of our room.

That's when I realize that privacy was another thing that left with Dad.

I don't go after her. The mad and sad and worried feelings have taken over my brain. My whole body feels like it's shutting down. My eyes are heavy and tired. I lie on my bed for a while, the light streaming in through the shutters.

Knock, knock.

I open my eyes, look at the time on my phone, and realize I fell asleep.

Knock. Knock.

"Come in," I say, assuming it's my mom. But it's Pickle. "Mom said I had to wait until you said I could come in if the door was closed. She also said you were sad," she says, holding out a jar of pickles. "Want one?" she asks.

I sit up and take a pickle. "Thanks. I'm sorry I yelled at you."

"Mom said it was okay to tell you that I don't like it when you yell even when you're sad."

"That's fair."

"I know what we can do that will make you not sad anymore," she says, grabbing my hand. "We can be Super Sisters." She ties her lime-green cape around her neck and hands me my orange one.

I wipe my eyes and put on my sister cape.

Pickle smiles big. Like she doesn't care that I'm weird or mess up stuff or lost Fearless Fred.

We spend the rest of the day downstairs at Hillview Vet. Mom's working, so I'm in charge of Pickle.

"Let's make more of those," she says, pointing to the stack of KAT posters I forgot were being stored here. The march is on Sunday. It feels like the whole town is going. Well, almost the whole town.

I don't want to think about the march that was my idea. The one that's hurting my friend.

"I have a better plan. Let's visit Superman." We reroute to the greenhouse to get him some leafy plants and wind our way to his cage. Pickle hands me her library book *Pink Is for Blobfish,* and I read to her and Superman.

Then we visit Flame and Wilbur. I think they're both easier to talk to than any two-legged human.

My phone rings. It's Prisha. I tell her what's going on while Pickle and I wind our way back to the waiting room.

"Everyone knows," I say, biting the inside of my cheek. "Cooper's mad. Pretty sure he hates me."

"Well, I don't hate you," Prisha says.

I smile. "I don't think it's fair that he's so mad. He knew Dear Student was someone at the school and that it was a secret."

"Exactly. It's not fair. That's what I've been telling you." She laughs. "At least I know you're listening even though there are thousands of miles between us."

I exhale. "But maybe it doesn't matter if it's fair. He's still angry."

"Maybe you need to stop worrying about Cooper and start thinking about what matters to you."

"But he's my friend."

"I get that. But real friends stick around," she says. "Just look at me. You can't get rid of me."

We both laugh.

"You can't be afraid to say or do the things that are important to you."

"You sound like my dad."

"Think about it. And just be you, okay? I promise you're awesome. And no matter what happens, know I love you."

"Love you back."

She's telling me about the rehearsals for *Hairspray* when I hear Barry Grayson's voice on the television behind Malcolm. "Breaking news. We're here at Beautiful You, where someone has graffitied hate speech in big black letters across the front of the building."

48

This Is Me

I wish I were a caterpillar that could fold into a cocoon and hide from the world.

I tell Prisha what I just heard on the news. "I didn't do this," I say, guilt and fear worming into my words.

"Of course you didn't," she says, like it's obvious.

But my worries ripple. "Maybe I started people thinking. And some of those thinking people got angry. And then they did this."

"It's still *not* your fault," she says.

I exhale a big breath I didn't realize I was holding. "Why is doing one good thing so complicated?"

"Don't know. But I do know that being complicated isn't a reason not to do something that matters to you."

I wonder if this is how my dad feels.

We talk for a while. Between trying to convince me that I'm not responsible for the graffiti on Beautiful You, she tells me the play's going great. Then she sends me a pic of her in full costume.

I tell her I know she'll be amazing. Before we hang up, I ask, "What do you think I should do about all of this stuff?"

"Not sure. What would Dear Student do?" she says.

I'm thinking about Prisha's words when my phone pings. It's Logan. She heard the news too. Neither of us wanted this. And if I believe Prisha, this is not our fault. But I can't shake the guilt that's wrapping around me.

I think about what Prisha asked me. What matters to me? What would Dear Student do? What can I do?

I open my computer and type.

Dear Students,

As some of you now know, I'm the secret voice behind Dear Student. It was my job to give advice about what to wear or what to do if you hate math or are stranded on an island.

And if I'm being totally honest—since that's really

the whole point of this letter—I was supernervous to do this. But I did it.

I did it because my dad said I needed to seize the day. I did it because this one thing was something I could do anonymously and, for me, it's way easier to be invisible. And I did it because someone believed I could give good advice. The kind that's honest and from the heart.

So I said yes. And then something amazing happened. Lots of you liked my advice. Even took my advice. But, not everyone. For those who didn't agree, that's totally okay. For those who didn't agree and are mad about the advice I gave, I'm sorry it hurt you.

But I'm not sorry for what I said. Either as Dear Student or as me. I was asked to be honest. And I was. I was asked to give advice from my heart. And I did. I never wanted to hurt anyone. I'm sorry you didn't like what I had to say. But I'm not sorry for having an opinion that's different from yours.

We don't have to think the same or believe the same things to be friends. But we do always have to be kind to each other. And respectful of each other.

As Dear Student, I've learned the most fearless (and frightening) thing I can do is be myself.

So, Hillview Middle, I'm done hiding.

This is me.

Signed,

Autumn Blake

PS: I'll be at Beautiful You tomorrow morning before school, scrubbing the hate off the building. Join me!

I touch the orange ribbon that's woven into my braid, inhale, and hit Send.

49

No More Secrets

I don't eat breakfast, even though Mom's making Dad's famous cheese eggs.

"Want your cape?" Pickle asks, drowning her eggs in ketchup.

I shake my head.

"Want to borrow mine?" she offers, holding out the corners of the lime-green cape that's tied around her neck.

I shake my head again.

This morning my letter as Autumn Blake came out in a special early online edition of *The Express*. So today I head out with no superhero cape. No secret identity.

Time to be seen.

Time to be me.

Last night, after I hit Send, I called Prisha and read her my letter. She gave it five out of five stars and told me she wished she still lived in Hillview so she could be with me today.

Then I called Logan. I needed my new friend to see me. The real me.

She said the letter was amazing. Then, "I should have trusted you. I should have just asked you that stuff I asked Dear Student."

"Why didn't you?"

"Don't know. I think maybe I was embarrassed."

I didn't know she got embarrassed.

Then she said, "Autumn, you're the brave one," which made me feel all the feels.

We talked a bit longer and agreed there'd be no more secrets between us.

I head out with Mom, Malcolm, and Pickle to Beautiful You. When we arrive, no one's there. I tell myself it doesn't matter. Doing the right thing doesn't need an audience.

We scrub the hate off the wall. We're making progress when someone taps my shoulder. It's Mr. Baker, who's wearing a shirt that says THE KIND THING IS ALWAYS THE RIGHT THING. He gives me a warm smile. "It took a lot of courage to write that letter, Autumn."

"Thanks," I say.

When I turn around, Cooper's walking toward the wall.

I head over to him. "I never meant for this to happen."

"I know," he says. Then, "Look, I'm sorry about the things I said at school yesterday. I'm just worried about my mom. And other stuff."

I nod and take a deep breath in. *Be brave. Even if your brave is mixed with a little weird and a lot of worry.* "I'm sorry too, about the whole Dear Student thing. But I'm, um, not sorry for what I said."

"You're not very good at this apologizing thing," Cooper says, pulling down his Wizards cap.

I keep going. "I think Beautiful You is wrong, so I'm doing something about it. You don't have to agree with me."

He shakes his head. "You don't get it. My feelings about all of this have nothing to do with agreeing or disagreeing with you."

"We don't have to think the same to be friends," I say, remembering that Prisha loves to dance.

"Beautiful You is the company where my mom finally got a job." He pauses.

I sigh.

"And if the march or just all this hate causes the

business to shut down, then my mom loses her job and I lose Mr. Magoo."

"Wait. Why?" He never said anything about Mr. Magoo.

"We can't afford to keep him."

"But we can do another whoopie pie stand or lemonade stand or hot dogs. Everyone loves hot dogs. I'll help you raise the money."

"It's not enough, Autumn," he says, sadness dripping from every word.

"This isn't fair," I say.

"That's the part you don't get. Sometimes stuff isn't fair. It doesn't always work out."

Just then a woman with eyes the color of chestnuts walks over to us. "Hello," she says.

"Hi, Mom," he says, then turns to me. "This is my friend Autumn."

We're still friends. The light in my heart flickers on.

"Nice to meet you," Cooper's mom says.

Then I spy Logan's sparkly sneakers walking toward me.

Cooper moves away, but he turns back around and says, "Find me later. There's something else I need to talk to you about." He heads to the wall with his mom and I walk over to Logan.

She hugs me.

I hug her back, turn to the small crowd gathering, and say in a voice I didn't know I had, "Now let's clean this building!"

We scrub for a few hours. Logan has to leave early, but most people stay until we remove enough of the ugly words that no one can read them. Before we go, the police come by. I hear them tell Mom and Mr. Baker they have a few leads from the street cameras in the neighborhood. Then they thank us for helping the community. That makes my insides glow. I wonder if this is what fireflies feel like all the time.

"You ready?" I hear Cooper's mom ask him.

"I need a minute," he says, walking over to me. "Good job today."

"Thanks," I say. "I'm glad you came." I put down the scrubbing brush.

"Yeah. Me too."

"And, you're right. Your mom does seem cool."

He smiles, then coughs in that nervous way. "Look, we're friends, so there's something you should know."

"What?" The worries creep up my spine.

"People aren't always what they seem."

"What does that mean?" This sounds like one of those riddles I'd never figure out.

"Some people say they're your friend, but they don't act like a friend when you're not around."

This isn't any clearer. "What are you talking about?"

"Pin the Tail on the Iguana."

My stomach clenches. "How do you know about that?" It was the game from my birthday party with Pickle. Something he shouldn't know about. Something no one should know about except a bunch of five-year-olds.

"Same way I and everyone else found out that you were Dear Student."

I feel like I'm sinking underwater.

Cooper says nothing for a minute, which feels like an hour.

Then he turns to me and says, "It was Logan."

50 The Loud Boom

I thought when my world crashed, I'd hear the deafening blow. The loud boom.

But I was wrong.

Turns out, it's silent.

Like drowning.

I leave Cooper and head straight to Hillview Vet. Superman's eating collard greens from the greenhouse. I pull out my frayed notebook. I'm wondering what Kiko would do, what I should do, when a short, round man with lots of curls comes rushing through the front door out of breath. "I saw online you have Mr. Bojangles."

Malcolm looks at the computer. "I'm sorry, sir. We don't have any animal by that name here."

The man's hands fly in the air. "Oh, right. In the video you call him something else. Something I can't remember. He's a beautiful iguana. Looks like this." The man pulls up a photo on his phone.

"Oh, that's Superman," I hear Malcolm say.

I go over to the front desk. "You're Superman's dad?"

He puts his hands over his heart. "I love that's what you named him. Yes, I'm Nick."

"Where have you been?" I ask.

"I'm a photographer for a wildlife magazine and was working on a story on the rain forests in Costa Rica." He takes out his business card and hands it to Malcolm. "My brother was checking on Mr. Bojangles while I was away. And one day he went into my house to feed him and Mr. Bojangles was gone. I didn't even know that had happened. I was in an area where there was no Wi-Fi. When I finally spoke to my brother, he was panicked. I scoured online and saw your video."

I think back to the day when Cooper and I made that video. That was before my life unraveled like a giant ball of yarn.

"We brought him here when his tail was accidentally run over by a boy on a bicycle," Autumn says.

"Is he okay? Can I see him?"

Malcolm nods. "He's great now. He's gotten a lot of love." Malcolm smiles at me.

"Thank you for taking care of him," the man says to me as he goes over to Mr. Bojangles, a.k.a. Superman.

My heart feels a smidgen brighter. Stronger.

I'm heading back to the sea of plastic chairs when I hear the door chime and recognize the voice talking to Malcolm.

"Something's wrong with Snow White."

I glance over and Logan looks up.

My heart thunders with hurt.

She runs over to me. "I'm so glad you're here," she says, tears staining her face.

I don't want to feel bad for you.

"Snow White started wheezing really loudly. So my mom and I brought her here."

"I'm sure my mom will know how to fix her." I start to walk away.

"Wait," Logan says, touching my arm. "Will you sit with me? Please? My mom dropped me off. She had to do something at her office. She'll be back soon."

I want to say no. But I can't. I follow her to the waiting room. I sit quietly for a while. I don't have the words to say what my heart is feeling.

Then I think about saving Superman and take in all the courage Logan said I have. "Was it you?" My voice trembles.

"Was what me?" she asks.

"Did you tell everyone I was Dear Student?" I say, the disbelief slipping into every syllable.

She puts her head in her hands. "You don't understand."

"That's true," I say, trying hard to hide my hurt. "I don't."

"I didn't mean to out you. Not really."

This isn't helping.

"I wasn't even totally sure it was you. But no one else I know loves strawberry banana cream pie and talks like an old person."

"What does that mean?" I say.

"No one our age says, 'I see the pickle you're in.' No one except you."

The spit pools in the back of my throat. I remember writing that in one of the most recent Dear Student letters.

"Look, I was mad at you," she says. "It happens with friends sometimes."

"About what?"

"You were ruining the whole march thing. *My* thing."

"It isn't *your* thing. It's the community's thing. No one owns it."

"You were all unsure and worried and being weird."

There's that word again.

"I wasn't being weird. I was trying to figure it out.

And I wasn't ruining anything. I just didn't want to hurt Cooper."

"Then I asked you, like, three times to do something with me and you said no." She stares down at her purple nail polish.

"I couldn't. I had stuff to do. I told you that."

"But then you were with that kid Cooper. Baking whoopie pies for his dog," Logan says.

"They weren't for his dog. They were to raise money to help pay for his dog. But what does that have to do with anything?"

"I told you my mom bailed. You of all people know what that feels like."

Her words feel like a vise, squeezing the air out of my lungs.

She pauses. "Why couldn't you have just asked me to help you guys?"

"You don't even like Cooper. Which makes it super confusing. I mean, am I supposed to invite you to do something with someone you've told me you think is weird and I shouldn't hang out with?" I ask.

Then, as if I just walked into a dark room and the lights turned on . . . "So it *was* you?" My mouth feels desert-dirt dry.

"I was sad and a little mad. So I told some people from school that it might be you. I didn't say it *was* you."

Is this an apology?

"And the Pin the Tail on the Iguana?" I ask.

"Come on, that was funny. I only told a few people. And even you have to admit that a middle-school party with a bunch of five-year-olds playing Pin the Tail on the Iguana is kind of hysterical."

Not funny.

Not funny.

Not funny.

"I should have said something to you when it all blew up," Logan admits.

I nod.

"I guess we were both keeping secrets," she says.

My mind spins. I need to focus. Find the words. Unstick them. And say them.

I look at my friend. "This is not the same. I didn't tell you about Dear Student because secrecy was part of the job." The next words are harder to untangle. "But the whole point of your secret was to hurt me."

Not the same.

51

Sorry Doesn't Fix This

Turns out Snow White is going to be okay. All she needs is some medicine.

But I wonder if Logan and I are going to be okay. If we can be fixed. If that's what I even want. After everything, I don't know. Mom says it's all right not to know. Which is another confusing thing. Especially when you like knowing things.

On Sunday morning before the march, Pickle and I surprise Mom with a package wrapped in orange paper. "It's not something dead, is it?" Mom asks.

Pickle and I laugh. "Nope. Nothing dead," I say. "We promise." Slowly Mom opens the gift. And sitting in the middle of the box is a happy-face yellow cape for the bravest person I know.

Mom drapes her cape over her shoulders. "I love it!" she says, a small tear rolling down her cheek.

I hold Pickle's hand. Then I tie my cape around my neck and Pickle does the same with hers. And as we head to the march, we're two Super Sisters and one Super Mom. When we get to the start, there are already swarms of people lined up. I spy Logan with her parents, but I don't go over. Being with her now fills my heart with sands of sad and mad.

I see Jules, Evie, and Maya, Reilly and Maisy, Zahara and the kids from Your Voice Matters, Mr. Baker, lots of random people from school who look sort of familiar, grown-ups from town, the guy who cuts Mom's hair, even Nick and Mr. Bojangles are here.

I'm not sure how it starts, but everyone links arms and holds signs as we walk peacefully together.

"If animals hurt, we hurt."

"Kindness matters."

"Protect our four-legged, feathered, and furry friends."

"Give voice to the voiceless."

The march circles around the park, down the hill, through the town. We chant and stay connected the entire time. I'm proud this march is happening. Proud I'm a part of it. And proud I'm wearing my cape with my Super Sister and Super Mom.

Pickle holds my hand as we walk. Until her legs get tired, then she hops on my back. When we stop for water, Logan comes over.

Pickle slides off my back and hugs her. She thinks Logan's like Wonder Woman. She doesn't know that Logan hurt me. On purpose.

"I'm sorry," Logan says. "I should have said it before."

Sorry doesn't fix this.

"I also wanted to tell you that I took Dear Student's advice. Or, your advice. Or whatever. And talked to my mom."

"Oh."

"My mom told me I was wrong and needed to apologize to you." Logan twirls her hair around her finger tightly.

"Is that why you're saying you're sorry?"

"No. I'm saying it because I am." She looks down at her sparkly sneakers. "I also talked to her about me and that I get sad sometimes being alone when she's out changing the world. Even though I'm glad she's doing it and I know it's really important. Maybe even more important than me."

My heart sinks. For Logan and for me.

"What did she say?"

"She said there are sacrifices you make when you commit to something bigger than yourself."

Sounds like something Dad would say.

"She said even when the cause is worthy, sacrifices can feel hard and heavy." She blinks back the tears that are fighting to fall.

"What did you say?"

"I told her I get it, but sometimes I hate being alone." Her mouth twists. "Then she said she was sorry, and we shared a black raspberry sundae with lots of chocolate syrup and watched the documentary on Ruth Bader Ginsburg."

"I'm glad you talked to her. And I'm glad there was ice cream. And Ruth," I say.

She smiles. "Thanks." Then, "Are we okay?"

I inhale big. There's still mad and hurt and empty space where trust used to be. But I look at my friend with the sparkly sneakers. "Maybe."

52

Best Kind of Weird

The day after the march, I think about Cooper and his mom and Mr. Magoo. I know marching was the right thing to do for me. But I never wanted to hurt my friend. And I have an idea.

I open my laptop, type an email, put on my cape, and hit Send. Now I wait for the owner of Beautiful You to respond. I know the owner never got back to Logan when she first emailed before the march. But I'm hoping that since the march got lots of attention, the owner will agree to talk with me.

I grab my notebook and write what Kiko does next.

She leaned down and handed her friend his back-pack. Max got up and they walked to school. Together.

My phone pings.

My heart races. Fingers crossed it's from the owner of Beautiful You.

But it isn't. It's Logan. *Want to hang out? We can go online and read the stories about the march.* She texts like she didn't hurt me. On purpose.

No thanks, I text back. I don't want her to be alone. Or feel bad. Or sad. I'm glad she's sorry for what she did and I hope in time that'll be enough. Like it was with Kiko and Max.

I call Prisha. I had sent her pictures and a long text about the march and Logan. Today, I tell her about my idea and my email to Charlie Marks, owner of Beautiful You. And while she's screaming "I totally can't believe you did that!" my phone pings. This time it's not from Logan.

Dear Ms. Autumn Blake,

Thank you for reaching out to me, particularly at this time of protest. I would very much like to meet with you. My assistant will contact you shortly with all the details.

I look forward to meeting you.

Best,

Charlie Marks

"You did it!" Prisha says.

"Not yet."

"But you will," she says.

"How do you know?"

"Because you're brave and the best kind of weird."

We laugh and she sings me the song she's been practicing for *Hairspray*.

That Friday after school, I head out to meet Charlie Marks.

"Do you want me to come with you?" Mom asked me this morning.

I shake my head. "No. But thanks."

"What about me?" Pickle said.

"Not today."

The door to the office building has a security person standing out front. It makes my stomach feel wobbly.

I take a big breath in. I've got this.

I check in at the shiny black desk in the too-bright lobby. A man with a navy shirt that says BEAUTIFUL YOU directs me to the second floor. When I get off the elevator, a woman in patent-leather high heels, black hair, bright pink lipstick, and a bun greets me.

"You must be Autumn," she says.

I nod.

"Thanks for coming. I'm Charlie."

My eyebrows scrunch. In my head, Charlie was a tall man in a dark suit with a mean face.

She shows me to her office. It takes fifty-seven steps to get from the entrance to her office that has a candle that smells like vanilla and lots of photos of people. No pets. Which is funny when I think of Hillview Vet and all the animal pictures hanging on the walls.

She sits behind her desk.

Okay. Now is the time. Find your words.

I say nothing.

"I know you wanted to meet with me," she says with a warm smile. "But first I wanted to thank you for cleaning the building after the graffiti incident."

I nod and stare at the wall behind her. It's pale yellow. I think of Prisha. And Fearless Fred. "I'm sorry that happened to your building."

"Thank you."

"I wanted to meet to, um, tell you that I don't like your policy about using animals to test the safety of your cosmetics." Keep going. This is what you practiced. "I have a pet guinea pig named Spud, and my mom's the vet at the Hillview Veterinary Clinic in town." I rub my *hamsa* charm. "I marched to protest your animal policy. I don't think it's right for a company to hurt animals."

Charlie nods as I talk. She lets me share all the things I'm mad about without interrupting. Which is the second surprising thing about the meeting. Usually when people disagree, they interrupt to tell you why you're wrong. But she doesn't. She listens.

My voice gets stronger. "And if Beautiful You were to change its policy to become a company that protects animals instead of testing on them, that would be a great selling point." I thought of this idea in the shower this morning while I was using my new watermelon-smelling conditioner.

Knock, knock.

A girl about Pickle's age comes in with pigtails and two missing teeth.

"This is my daughter, Ella," Charlie says as Ella waves. "She's the reason I took your meeting. She saw the march, which led to lots of questions and hours of her not speaking to me." Charlie laughs. "And if you knew Ella, you'd know that's a huge deal."

"I told my mom she shouldn't work for a company that hurts animals. I told my mom I thought you were the bravest person ever and that when I grow up, I want to be just like you."

My face gets hot.

Charlie moves from behind her desk and stands closer to me. Her perfume smells like mango. "First, our company does no animal testing on products sold in the United States."

Mom and I talked about this last night while eating chicken Parm and the best garlic bread ever. "All your stuff for sale in the United States says 'cruelty-free.' And that's true. I guess. But since you also sell your stuff in countries that require testing, you still do some testing on animals."

Charlie nods. "But that changes today."

"Are you closing the business?" I ask nervously. I think about Cooper and know this isn't what I want anymore.

"No," she says.

I exhale.

"Our business practices are, however, evolving. My grandfather, the founder of this company, recently passed away. He trusted me to take the company in a new direction and that's what I plan to do. The business will open in Hillview, but we're fully committed to the complete elimination of animal testing." Charlie smiles at me and her daughter. “Increased awareness is a good thing. It makes people think.”

Ella smiles at me.

My insides burst with happiness. And something else. I think it’s courage.

I did it!

53

Apartment Number 9

I leave Beautiful You, stop home to pick something up, and then head out. I turn right and left down Lansdown Lane and go into Hillview Apartments. On the stairs, I pass an elderly man wearing a newsboy cap that looks like a hat from one of Dad's postcards. I'm relieved that I'm not stopping on the second floor. While it doesn't smell like cabbage, it does smell like brussels sprouts. And I hate brussels sprouts even more than I hate cooked cabbage.

Two more flights of stairs. As I get closer to apartment number 9 on the fourth floor, my happy feeling dips behind a pile of worries. What if Cooper is mad I didn't ask him first? What if I'm wrong and his mom is out of a job and Mr. Magoo can't stay with them? What if I fixed nothing?

I stop walking. Turn back around. Away from number 9 and sit on the top step of the landing. I count and breathe and imagine a room full of baby guinea pigs, but the prickly feeling snakes down my back.

I count again.

Footsteps come up the stairs. It's a couple and their two little boys. They smile. I nod.

More footsteps. I don't look up. I don't want to do the polite nice-to-see-you thing. Instead I stare at the mud stuck on the step below me.

"Autumn?"

The footsteps belong to Cooper.

He sits down next to me. "Glad you got my text," he says.

I look at my phone. Missed text from Cooper: *You around? Meet me at #9?*

"Why did you want to meet?" I ask, scratching off the remaining purple nail polish on my ring finger.

"I heard the march was a success," he says. "Congrats."

"Thanks." I smile and stare at my friend.

Just tell him.

"Um, I have more great news." I wait a beat to take in all the breath I need to keep talking. "I just came from meeting with the owner of Beautiful You. They're staying open *and* changing their animal testing policies." I exhale.

"I know. My mom told me. Some company-wide email went around to all the employees," he says.

"And Mr. Magoo?"

"I get to keep him."

A heap of grateful air escapes my lungs.

"But I still have to take care of him. So, are you up for making more whoopie pies?"

I hold up the jar of peanut butter I grabbed from home on my way here. "I'm ready."

His smile slips out.

And my happy feeling slides back in.

"I think we're going to need a name for our business," he says, standing up.

"I've got the perfect one. Fearless Fred's Famous Whoopie Pies."

54 Brave Like Me

This morning I sit at the desk with the nicks in the wood and write on the last page of my orange-and-purple-check notebook. I realize that making my words small was making me small. And I don't want to be small anymore.

I close my notebook and pull from the drawer the postcard I made. On the front is a photograph of Mom, Pickle, and me from the march. Two Super Sisters and one Super Mom holding hands and wearing capes. It's time to find Fearless Fred and share how I really feel. All of it.

I flip over the postcard and write:

Dear Dad,

Since you left, I've felt all the feels. Sometimes that's been superconfusing. Like when you say it was brave to leave. I get the courage it takes to seize the day. But I don't think I'll ever agree that leaving was brave. To me, leaving feels like sadness and missing and an empty hole in my heart. It's staying that's hard. I think that's the real brave thing.

I also realized that I can feel lots of different things at the same time. Like I can be kind of mad at you, love you, miss you huge, and know I'm going to be all right. Even if you stay in Ecuador. Even if the temporary house without the lilac bushes is really my forever home. Not because I'm brave like you. But because I'm brave like me.

Don't forget to seize the day!

Your Loving and Brave Daughter,
Autumn Blake

Fearless Fred's Famous Whoopie Pies

With Peanut Butter Cream

INGREDIENTS

Yummy Chocolate Cakes

1 cup buttermilk (if you don't have buttermilk, you can use 1 tablespoon lemon juice or white vinegar and 1 cup of regular milk)

1 teaspoon vanilla

2 cups all-purpose flour

1/2 cup cocoa powder

1-1/4 teaspoons baking soda

1 teaspoon salt

1 large egg

1 stick unsalted butter, softened

1 cup packed brown sugar

Delicious Peanut Butter Cream

1 stick unsalted butter

1-1/4 cups confectioners' sugar

2 cups Marshmallow Fluff

1-1/4 cups peanut butter (smooth or crunchy)

1/4 cup water

How to Bake the Cakes

Preheat oven to 350° F. Stir vanilla and buttermilk (if using—see allergen notes below) in a bowl. Mix flour, cocoa, baking soda, and salt in a separate bowl. Beat the butter and brown sugar in a third bowl until fluffy. (If you don't have an electric mixer, mix by hand.) Add egg to butter/sugar mixture and beat. Then lower speed on electric mixer and mix in wet and dry ingredients a little bit at a time. Mix until smooth.

Drop batter in 1/4-cup heaps onto 2 greased baking sheets, leaving about an inch of space between heaps. Bake for about 11 to 13 minutes. Tops should feel springy. Remove from oven to a rack and let cool.

How to make the delicious cream

Beat together the butter, confectioners' sugar, Marshmallow Fluff, peanut butter and water in a bowl with an electric mixer until smooth. Again, if you don't have an electric mixer, no worries. Just mix by hand.

Putting it all together

Lay 2 cakes on a plate. Spread the delicious inside onto the flat side of each cake and put them together.

Now . . . take a giant bite and enjoy!

Allergy-Friendly Tips

If you are gluten free (like me!), simply substitute gluten-free flour for all-purpose flour.

If you are dairy free (also like me!), simply use your favorite butter substitute. Substitute coconut milk and 1 tablespoon lemon juice or white vinegar for buttermilk.

If you are both gluten and dairy free, substitute all of the above.

If you are nut free, eliminate the peanut butter, add a teaspoon of vanilla, and have a delicious traditional creamy inside.

Fearless Fred's Famous Whoopie Pies were inspired by recipes at Epicurious and The Cookie Rookie.

Acknowledgments

In *Dear Student,* Autumn finds her voice and, in the process, herself. Her journey is championed by people who believe in her. I'm grateful to be surrounded by people who believe in me and in this story.

Topping this list is my family. To my husband, James, I am ever grateful for you, for us, and for our forever. Thanks for always believing in me. To my son Joshua and new daughter-in-law, Sophie, I am grateful for your love and support. And for that time at the Cape sitting around the kitchen table when you read the *Dear Student* proposal and said you really liked the story. You have no idea how those words carried me when doubt crept in. To my son Gregory, I am grateful for our writing sessions over Skype, for your unwavering belief in my ability to tell this story, and for all the times we brainstormed. Couldn't have done it without you! And I'm so thankful for the love and cheers from both you and Shannon.

Dad, Sandy, and Gia, hugs and love for always cheering me on. You fill my heart. I am so lucky to be your daughter.

Scott and Daniel, this book is for you. I'm so grateful to have you as my big brothers. And I forgive you for farting on my pillow as kids. All kidding aside, thanks for always having my back. I love you both with all my heart.

Scott, Rena, Ben, Jess, Gabe, Gen, Sam, Maddie, Daniel, Faith, Eli, Ari, Asher, Joan, Larry, Emily, Matthew, Andrew—how lucky I am to be part of this rock-star family. So much love for all of you.

To my amazing agent, Andrea Cascardi, a huge heap of thanks for believing in Autumn's story and in me. Your feedback was beyond helpful and your support and encouragement were incredibly meaningful. We make a great team! Thank you times a million!

To my rock-star editor, Wendy Loggia, wow! I have loved working with you. Your input was spot-on and truly helped me find the special sauce in Autumn's story. A huge thanks to you and a special shout-out to Alison Romig for all her incredible help getting this story across the finish line and Simini Blocker for my amazing cover. So much gratitude to the incredible team at Delacorte Press and Penguin Random House. Feeling grateful to be a part of this family.

Joan, an added heap of gratitude for reading and

helping me infuse and navigate plot. While nothing exploded in the story, I learned so much from our Cape writing retreat! And I loved our time together writing, sharing, and being sisters.

Victoria Coe and Sarah Aronson, thank you for reading and rereading and helping me stay true to Autumn and her heart. And for guiding me when I needed it most. Especially when I shared my outline that simply said, "Something great happens here!" Grateful for you both!

Padma Venkatraman, a million thanks for your kindness and friendship, and for reading my story with heart and sensitivity. Your input was helpful, and your blurb makes my heart so happy!

Laurie and Reesa, thank you for your forever friendship and for reading even when I was nervous to share my story and my heart.

Shanti Gonzales, so grateful for your input and for reading and sharing your thoughts. I loved our Zoom chats. Truly meant so much to me.

In addition to love and support, there was much research that went into creating this story. Authenticity, respect, and accuracy of detail are the cornerstones of my writing. And how lucky I am for the gracious generosity of those who shared their expertise.

Dr. Kathleen Trainor, I am so grateful for your guidance and thoughtful input. As a senior psychologist at the Child Psychiatry Clinic at Massachusetts General Hospital who treats children and adolescents with anxiety-based disorders, founder of the TRAINOR Center, and author of *Calming Your Anxious Child: Words to Say and Things to Do* (2016), you helped ensure that Autumn's social anxiety felt authentic.

A huge thank-you to Congressman Don Beyer of Virginia, who sponsored the bill Humane Cosmetics Act of 2019 (congress.gov/bill/116th-congress/house-bill/5141/text); his intern Ari Hawkins, who was kind enough to call me back; and Connor Vargo, who deals with all things animal welfare and who graciously took the time to share his insight about the bill and the world of cosmetics and animal testing. Appreciate you all!

Stephen Ayer of Jabberwock Reptiles in Winchester, Mass., I am grateful for your knowledge and willingness to answer my questions about all things iguanas and snakes. So helpful.

David Jarmul, a two-time Peace Corps volunteer and author of the book *Not Exactly Retired,* thank you for your input on your experience as an older Peace Corps volunteer. Your insight was invaluable. And to the Peace Corps, keep doing the great work. We truly are better together!

Educators' kindness is limitless. A huge thank-you to Spanish teachers Chandra Erickson and Diane Mancini, who gave incredible input on the Spanish-translation portion of Autumn's story. And to Heather Palmer, the gracious librarian who connected us.

Thank you to Alex Seegers, kid reader and editor extraordinaire, for making sure Autumn, Logan, and Cooper stayed true to being kids. Kids can teach us. All we need to do is listen. Huge thanks, Alex!

To Anna Kontos, grateful for you, my friend. Thanks for always saying yes. Loved working on the curriculum guide together. Truly love doing anything together.

Rayna Freedman—warrior, reader, educator—grateful for your insight and input on the curriculum guide. Love collaborating with you and learning from each other.

"Thank you" is truly not big enough to express the immeasurable gratitude I feel for all those who believed in me and this story. And for all who will pick it up to read it. My gratitude is boundless!

To educators and librarians, I am grateful for all you do every day. You offer kindness. You touch hearts. You open minds. Thank you!

To my readers, you have my heart and my gratitude. And as Prisha says, just be you! You are special. You are brave. And you will always be enough.

Your friend,

Elly

About the Author

Elly Swartz grew up in Yardley, Pennsylvania. She studied psychology at Boston University and received her law degree from Georgetown University Law Center. Elly lives in Massachusetts and is happily married with two grown sons, a beagle named Lucy, and a pup named Baxter Bean. *Finding Perfect,* called "a clear, moving portrayal of obsessive-compulsive disorder" by *Publishers Weekly,* was her debut novel. She is also the author of *Smart Cookie* and *Give and Take,* novels for middle-grade readers.

ellyswartz.com